a Very Merry HOCKEY HOLIDAY

novella

a Very Merry HOCKEY HOLIDAY

novella

TONI ALEO

Formatted by Tianne Samson with E.M. Tippetts Book Designs

The Bellevue Bullies Series

Boarded by Love
Clipped by Love **(early 2015)**
Hooked by Love (late 2015)

The Assassins Series

Taking Shots
Trying to Score
Empty Net
Falling for the Backup
Blue Lines
Breaking Away
Laces and Lace
A Very Merry Hockey Holiday
Overtime (Spring 2015)

Standalone

Let it be Me

Taking Risks Series

The Whiskey Prince
Becoming the Whiskey Princess (Due out 2015)

Happy Holidays, Assassin fans.
I love you.
This book is for you.

Lucas & FALLON

Lucas Brooks was a very lucky man.

Or at least he thought he was.

According to everyone at Rocky Top Wines though, he was crazy not only to be married but also to be completely and utterly in love with his wife, who was currently a crazy pregnant lady. While he didn't share their sentiments, he didn't miss the "poor bastard" looks he received as he made his way toward his wife's office in a hurry. He had tried calling Fallon at least six times before he arrived to get her for their eldest son, Aiden's, game but she was ignoring her phone. Like she always did when she was working. She knew he was coming though, and he planned to get on to her, but first things first was to get her out of the office and into the car.

He knew it was going to be a struggle, which was why he offered to pick her up. Not only did she hate the cold, but she was obsessing over the New Year's party that Rocky Top Wines was throwing for the Assassins team and he wished she wouldn't. Even without the added stress of the party, she was also only a week out from having their newest addition, a little girl. Which meant that Fallon was in full-bitch mode. He knew this. The kids knew this. Her family knew this. Everyone did. The only thing was, Lucas didn't care. They had a hockey game to get to, and hockey came before bitch mode and parties.

Hockey came before everything.

Reaching for the door, he paused when someone said, "I wouldn't do that."

Lucas looked over at Fallon's assistant Rob and chuckled. "Is she really that bad?"

Rob looked as if he had seen a ghost as he nodded slowly. "She is on a whole other level, Lucas. She told me that if I didn't get her Peppermint Oreos by lunch, I wasn't getting a holiday bonus!"

"I thought I stocked you up?" Lucas asked quietly, coming toward his desk.

"She ate them all!"

"I got you fifty packs!" Lucas yelled, shocked. "She ate fifty packs?"

"Dude, have you seen her ass? There's fifty packs worth of Oreos."

Lucas glared. "Don't talk about her like that; I like her ass."

"You would," he said with a roll of his eyes. "But me, I'm mad. She said my bow tie was stupid and that I shouldn't wear pants this tight because it was distracting. So really, she shouldn't talk to me like that," he said with a flair of his hand before waving Lucas off. "But whatever. I warned you. Go get eaten by Pregnantasaurus Rex."

Lucas scoffed. "That's funny."

"Ain't gonna be funny when she bites your head off for whatever reason she can think of."

"Probably 'cause I knocked her up," Lucas said with a wink.

But Rob didn't think Lucas was funny. The two had gotten close over the years. Rob was Fallon's sidekick and Lucas trusted him completely. He looked out for his beautiful wife, especially when she was with child. Fallon might threaten to take his bonus, but he would make sure Rob had a hefty check in his stocking for Christmas.

With a glare, Rob said, "I want to bite your head off for that."

Lucas laughed before pushing the door open to find his beautiful wife working hard behind her desk. She always stunned him when he saw her. Her hair was up in a high bun, her makeup done flawlessly, and her lips ever so plump and perfect. But he didn't miss the scowl on her face. Looking up from her desk, she glared before looking down at the clock.

"Shit," she muttered, going to her computer and clicking around like crazy, probably since she knew he would physically pick her up and drag her out of the office without letting her finish. She had till he got to her before he would shut the computer and make her leave.

Giving her time, he smiled as he asked, "Is that how you greet your loving husband?"

Her brow furrowed more before she shut down her computer. "I don't like you today."

"Do you ever like me?" he teased as she stood, her large belly straining beneath the sweater dress she wore. She was swollen from head to toe, but still she wore heels.

Crazy Pregnantasaurus Rex. He was going to use that more often.

"I wonder that sometimes," she snapped, moving her hair out of her face. "I can't even remember the reason I married you or continually make children with you."

He knew she didn't mean any of it, she was just…pregnant.

"'Cause I'm good in bed," he said with a wink and she glared.

"Ugh, I am so stressed out and my body aches and I really don't want to go sit in the rink because it hurts my back and ugh, Lucas, stop looking at me like that!"

He smiled. "You look beautiful," he cooed at her as she waddled toward him.

She rolled her eyes. "If you think fat is beautiful, then yeah, I'm that."

"Stop," he barked at her as she slid her arms into the jacket he held open for her. "You're scaring the employees, the kids, hell, everyone."

"But you," she challenged and he grinned.

"Except me. I know how to handle you. This isn't my first rodeo."

"Well, it will be your last," she warned as she let out a breath.

Kissing her neck, he wrapped his arms around her waist, his hands barely touching as he massaged his growing child. Kissing her again, he chuckled before whispering, "Did you know that I think you are the most gorgeous woman in the world?"

He saw her cheeks pull back in a small smile, but he knew it wasn't that easy. "You have to say that so I'll continue to sleep with you."

He chuckled against her jaw before dusting it slowly with kisses. "Never. You'll sleep with me no matter what."

"Maybe," she grumbled and he grinned, kissing her neck again.

"And the reason you married me is because you are totally devoted to me," he whispered again, his fingers dancing along where that was written along her wrist.

Totally devoted. It was their thing. Something he treasured.

Leaning against his face, she kissed his jaw. "You're right."

"I know, only happens sometimes," he said, kissing her again. Holding her tightly, he could feel every single bit of her tension. He hated that. She needed to be calm and stress-free. It couldn't be healthy for his new baby girl if her mother was stressed.

"What can I do to make you happy, Fallon?" he asked, his hands slowly going down her stomach to her thighs. She took in a sharp breath before leaning her head back against his shoulder, her body weight strong against him. It was nothing to him, though. He was pretty sure he could pick her up and take her against the wall, but of course, for the safety of their child, he wouldn't do that. But he would play. He would try to relieve some stress from his gorgeous wife.

He would do just about anything for her.

"I mean, I like the direction your hands are going, but aren't our children in the car?"

He nodded, tracing kisses up her neck. "They are, but Stella is sleeping and Aiden and Asher are playing their DSs. I can at least make you come real quick if it will make you happy."

Letting out a breath, she laced her fingers with his as she melted against him. Everyone thought she was crazy and mean, and yeah, she was, but with him, he could have her purring like a kitten in seconds. "Just being in your arms makes me happy."

He scoffed. "Liar. What do you want? Oreos and an orgasm?"

She giggled as she turned in his arms, wrapping her arms loosely around his neck. "That sounds like the mother of all plans, but I have no Oreos here and our babies are in the car. Let's go."

He wrapped his arms around her waist, her belly pressing against his growing erection. A contented grin sat on his face as he stared into his wife's eyes. It had been six years since he had gotten his love back, and to his surprise, it had come not only in the form of this gorgeous woman but also a little boy who held his world. The years had been great to them. They were very blessed with happiness, more children, and a marriage that no one could touch. She was still exquisite as ever, her caramel eyes piercing as her sweet mouth curved in such a delectable way. She was everything he ever needed, even when she was stubborn and difficult.

He loved that about her.

"Well, how about this, baby?" he started, gathering her tighter in his arms, pressing his nose into hers. "I get you home after the game, put on the bath since your back will be hurting, and then I'll get the kids to bed before making sweet love to you?"

"With Oreos?"

He grinned. "And I'll get you Oreos."

"You're the best husband in the world."

"I am," he said with a wink. "Now apologize to Rob before he quits on you."

"He would do no such thing," she said as they locked pinkies before walking out. "He loves me."

"The hell you say," Rob called, crossing his arms across his chest. "I'll love you again when you are done being pregnant. You know what? Can I get it in writing that this is the last kid or I'm quitting?"

Lucas chuckled as Fallon rolled her eyes. "Last one, I promise."

"I need that in writing. Really. I can't handle this anymore."

"I'm not that bad," Fallon said, glaring.

"Yes, you are," Lucas and Rob both said.

"But I love you," Lucas said to save his own ass, but Rob didn't care. He defiantly shook his head.

"I love you, but you are driving me insane. How many more days? Eight?"

Fallon held her stretched-to-the-max stomach with her other hand and let out a breath. "Seven, unless I can talk the doctor into getting her out on Monday."

"I'll be praying," Rob sang and Fallon smiled.

"Me too," Lucas said, kissing her cheek. "But we need to go."

They said bye to Rob before making their way out of the winery's business suites and toward their car that held their family. Opening the door for his wife, he helped her in as Stella cried out, "Mommy!"

"Hey, sugarplum," Fallon cooed as Lucas shut the door, running around to get in himself. It was colder than Antarctica, but with only thirty days till Christmas, it was expected and wanted. The kids were hoping for a white Christmas, but with Tennessee, it was always a surprise. He hoped for their sakes it was since he loved when his kids were happy, but he wasn't holding his breath.

Jumping into the truck, he said, "Jesus, it's cold."

"I hate it," Fallon complained under her breath and he smiled, but then he noticed as she moved, she cringed.

"You okay?" he asked, pulling out of the parking spot.

She shrugged. "My sides and back are killing me for some God-awful reason."

"Well, you are pregnant. You're not in labor, are you?"

She scoffed. "Please, Emery is not going anywhere. She is stubborn."

"Like her mother," he said with a knowing grin, but Fallon didn't seem to think he was funny.

"Mom, you're okay?" Aiden called from the back, and when Lucas looked in the mirror at his almost teenaged son, his heart hurt a bit. He'd missed so much of his life, but it just meant that he made every single second with Aiden count. He was his best friend, and Lucas was thankful for that. He was worried time would hurt them, but it was love at first sight for the two.

"Yeah, sweetheart, I'm sure it will pass," she said, waving him off. "You ready for your game?"

"He's gonna score me a goal!" Asher shouted out.

"No! He gonna score me a goal," Stella pouted and Lucas chuckled.

"I'll score you both a goal, and yeah, Mom, I'm ready," he said and that seemed to please his younger siblings as Lucas pulled into the sportsplex. He really was a great big brother; he was a great kid, his favorite. Not that he would tell any of the other kids that.

Pulling into a spot, he shut the car off and then got out to get Stella since

Aiden would help with Asher. Opening the back, he unhooked her car seat but saw that Fallon hadn't gotten out yet.

"Babe, you good?"

She nodded but didn't answer him, and that didn't sit well with him. As he threw Stella on his hip, she wrapped her little arms around his neck and kissed his cheek.

"Daddy, I love you."

Okay, maybe Stella was his favorite. He was completely wrapped around her sweet little finger. Smiling, Lucas kissed her nose and promised, "I love you way more, my sugarplum."

She giggled happily before he shut the door. Still eyeing Fallon through the window, he walked around the truck and watched as she cringed in pain. He knew right away that something was wrong.

"Hey Aiden, take Stella real quick for me."

"Everything okay, Dad?" he asked, taking Stella like he'd been asked. Lucas nodded as he threw the door open, looking in on his wife.

"You okay?"

Still not answering him, she sucked in a deep breath. Opening her eyes, she met his gaze, and he could see she was in more pain than she wanted to admit. "Yeah. Not sure what is going on. I think it might be Braxton Hicks."

Man, he hated those pains. She'd had them horribly with Asher and Stella, but it usually meant that it was almost time for the baby to come. "They suck and I know that, but it means she's coming."

"Yeah," she said with a nod, taking his hand, but as soon as her foot hit the ground, her eyes went wide.

"Fallon?" he asked.

"Mom?" Aiden asked then, taking a step forward, holding the back of her arm. She sucked in a deep breath, her nails digging into Lucas's forearm as she took another deep breath.

Looking up at them, she said, "I either just peed my pants or my water just broke."

"Oh crap," Aiden said, his eyes as wide as saucers.

"What's going on?" Asher asked, confused.

"Mommy! You have to use the toilet!" Stella scolded her, and all Lucas could do was laugh.

"Everyone back in the car! Time to have a baby!"

Fallon looked down at the little bundle of pink and felt completely euphoric.

Looking just like her daddy, Emery Elaine Brooks came in at a whopping nine pounds, Fallon's biggest baby, and was the most gorgeous baby she had ever seen. That was hard to say because she had three other beautiful children, but Emery was stunning. Her cheeks were the perfect color pink, her long black lashes kissed her cheeks, and her lips were bright red and currently puckered out as Fallon grinned down at her. She had been having pains all day but assumed it was indigestion or Braxton Hicks. Obviously she was wrong.

As she looked down at her sweet baby girl, she knew she had a lot of apologizing to do. Not only had she cussed out and threatened her assistant but she also had been a bitch to Audrey. She was always like that when she was pregnant, and while she loved her children, and more than loved making them with Lucas, she knew that Emery would be her last. There was no way she was going to put anyone else through nine months of crazy bitch-ass Fallon. Running her finger down Emery's jawline, she smiled.

"Momma's last sweet baby," she whispered, touching her lips to her forehead. The birth wasn't bad, really easy, fast, and with a grin, she thought maybe she was a pro. Nowhere near Elli Adler pro-status, but she had this. And just like that, she thought maybe she would have another, but then the door opened and her family filed in and she knew she had her hands full.

"Mommy! You have my sister?" Stella yelled through the room, startling Emery. Letting out a sound of distress, Emery cried as Fallon smiled and looked at her little firecracker. Stella had one volume. Loud. And Fallon was sure it came from Lucas's side of the family. Because she wasn't loud…

"Sugarplum, you can't be loud with the new baby," she said softly as Stella crawled into bed with her, looking down at her sister. Laying her head on Fallon's shoulder, Stella placed her little hand on her sister's chest and let out a sigh.

"I think I like her," she decided and Fallon's grin grew.

"Good, 'cause she's coming home with us," Aiden said, and Fallon looked up to meet the gaze of her eldest. He was so handsome, looking more and more like his father every day. He was out of the awkward stage, his teeth were nice and straight, his eyes as gray as storm clouds. The angles to his face were beautiful and so much like Lucas's. He was solid, already possessing a hockey player's body, and boy, could he play. He was almost thirteen, and it killed her to think of all the girls' hearts he was going to break. He was his father made over, and she couldn't be more thankful that Lucas was the man she'd chosen to have kids with. Yes, Aiden wasn't planned, but she wouldn't change who his father was. Back in the day was another story, but she'd been young and stupid. Now though, she knew who buttered her bread and that was Lucas Brooks.

Looking past her eldest, she saw that Lucas was carrying a sleeping Asher. Her little man didn't do mornings, and he was his momma's boy. He looked just like Fallon, and she took great pride in that since now three out of her four children were their father's miniatures. Lord, help them all if Emery was like Fallon. Stella was enough, and she honestly couldn't do a second girl like herself.

The horror.

Grinning, she said, "Is he awake?"

"You know he isn't, knocked out like you always are."

Lucas gave her a teasing grin, and she couldn't love him anymore than she already did. He'd been amazing through the birth. Ever so supportive and wonderful. He didn't even pass out this time! The other two times though, that was another story. Smiling, she mouthed, "I love you."

His whole face lit up as he leaned over to press his lips to hers. "I love you more," he whispered against her lips.

Conveniently, Asher woke up and pushed Lucas away before saying, "Ew, gross."

"You say that now, buddy, but you just wait," Lucas said with a wink. "Ask Aiden. He loves girls."

Aiden's face went deep scarlet before he complained. "Dad!"

Fallon laughed as Emery moved her arms up and stretched while Stella said, "Aw, it moves."

They all laughed. "It isn't an it, sugarplum; it's your sister," Fallon corrected her, kissing her temple.

"But you like me more, right?" she asked, her big gray eyes locking on Fallon's.

"No, she likes me more," Asher informed her.

"Yeah, right. I'm the first and her favorite," Aiden said proudly, winking at her as Lucas laughed.

"Last time, I checked, I was her favorite," Lucas offered, causing everyone to laugh and thankfully causing Stella to forget. But as they looked deep into each other's eyes, they knew the truth.

There was no favorite.

A couple days later…

Fallon laid Emery in her bassinet and picked up a tray of ornaments. Stella, Asher, and Aiden were already at work hanging ornaments while Lucas hung the stockings. Their home was almost fully decorated. Aiden and Lucas had spent the afternoon hanging the lights, while Asher and Stella helped with the inside décor. Sweet Emery slept through most of it, not that anyone was complaining. That girl had some lungs, and Fallon was more convinced that she was her daddy's girl.

Lucas was leaving later that night for a couple away games, and they wanted to have the house fully done. His mom, Molly, was coming into town in a week for Christmas and to meet her new granddaughter.

"Good job, Stella," Fallon doted, receiving a huge grin from her. They all talked happily about whatever came to mind as they dressed the tree with mismatched ornaments, but Fallon didn't care. Each ornament meant something. There were hockey sticks for Lucas, Asher, and Aiden, dance shoes for Stella, and wine for Fallon. Every time they went on vacation, she got an ornament for their tree. They had Disney ones and even Harry Potter ones since Aiden was still obsessed with the popular book series. It was a tree of love, and she didn't give two shits that it didn't match.

When they were all done, she smiled as she said, "Okay, here are all y'all's first ornaments. Let's hang them."

"What about Emery?" Stella asked as Fallon handed her her little pink star with her birthday on it and her name in pretty cursive.

"I haven't made it to the mall yet to have it made. She'll have it before Christmas. I promise."

"Actually," Lucas said, coming to them. "I went and got it for you."

Reaching into the tray she was holding, he held up another pink star with Emery's name on it, and for some dumb reason, Fallon's eyes welled up with tears.

"You did?"

He smiled, wrapping his arms around her waist. "I know how much it means to you to have the ornaments when we trim the tree, so the boys and I went to get it yesterday while you girls napped."

Looking over at Aiden and Asher, she found them grinning, and her heart felt as if it was going to come out of her chest as she slowly nodded. It was a tradition in her family to always have all the ornaments before you did the tree. She hadn't even wanted to decorate today, but Lucas pushed her to do it, and she was thankful for that. Wiping away a tear that fell, she shot them all a grin before handing the tray off to Lucas and then getting Emery. Her little eyes were wide as Fallon lifted her up and into the crook of her arm.

"Wanna hang your star, Emery? It's your ornament for your first Christmas," she asked as she made her way to where her family stood. Emery looked at her like she was speaking gibberish and spit up a little in response. Lucas reached over and wiped her mouth with a rag before kissing Fallon's cheek. Meeting his gaze, her heart skipped a beat before she moved toward him, kissing him softly on his lips. Still after all this time, he made the butterflies in her stomach go insane. Kissing her nose as they parted, he held up their first Christmas ornament, and she didn't think her heart could take it.

There was something about the ornament that made everything inside her go hot. Aiden had been away with Molly for the weekend, and they'd gone out to Gatlinburg for a mini-vacation. After touring the mountains and having a blast, they ended up in a little wedding chapel where they redid their vows, and one of the keepsakes was the ornament. After all that, they went back and had the hottest sex imaginable on the balcony of their huge cabin, the Smoky Mountains behind them as he drove her mad with orgasms. It had been one of her favorite trips to date and still gave her gooseflesh every time she thought about it.

"Our ornament," she whispered as he handed her Emery's.

"Yup, it's my favorite," he whispered back, kissing her ear. "Or maybe the things we did are."

She sucked in a deep breath as she nodded slowly. "Yes, I think I have to agree with you on that."

He shot her a wink before kissing her again. "Maybe once we get these monsters to bed, we can reenact that night."

She scoffed. "Sorry, buddy, you have a month before you get inside me."

"What are y'all talking about?" Aiden asked.

"It's weird; they are gross," Asher decided.

"I want to hang my ornament!" Stella yelled out, causing Fallon to grin.

Not moving, Lucas whispered, "As soon as I can, I'm going to make you come."

Her stomach clenched as she kissed his jaw. "Well, Lord knows, I won't stop you."

"I figured," he chuckled, kissing her again before they both looked back at their family. He had a huge grin on his face, and Fallon's heart thudded in her chest as she took in the beauty of him. He was like the finest wine and got better with age. He was gorgeous and all hers, but her favorite thing in the world was watching him watch his family. He was happy, and it was good to know it was because of her and the kids.

"Okay, guys, let's finish the tree," Lucas commanded, and with her new daughter in her arms, Fallon reached out, hanging Emery's star on one of the branches while everyone did the same. As they all stepped back, Lucas's fingers threaded with hers as Aiden leaned against her arm, Stella on his hip. Asher wrapped his arms around Fallon's butt and laid his head on her stomach as she let out a contented sigh.

Christmas was a time for giving, but what else could she ever get?

She had everything.

And then some.

Audrey & TATE

Watching the puck with intensity, Tate Odder was in set position as the Assassins' defense fought off the Bruins' offense. When Brooks took the puck up the ice, Tate stood up, shaking his limbs as he continued to watch. At any moment, the Bruins could get the puck back, but they wouldn't get it past. Not on his watch. When a Bruins player stole the puck and sailed past the defense and up ice on a breakaway, Tate grinned.

Here we go.

He deked left, but Tate knew he would and went right along with him, blocking the puck. To his surprise though, the little shit got the puck back and tried to go top shelf. The crowd roared, thinking their team was going to take the lead, but in a picture-worthy way, Tate caught it in his glove, bringing it in close to his chest, and the crowd wasn't happy. Tate was though, along with his teammates.

"Way to go, Odder," his captain, Shea, said as he tapped Tate's pad. "Great save."

"Thanks, Cap."

Handing the puck off to the ref, Tate got back in position and thought about winning.

And not about how miserable his wife was at home.

Surprisingly enough, Tate wasn't scored on even though he couldn't push away the thoughts of his wife. Audrey did well hiding her feelings, but he knew how much she was hurting and it was killing him. Any time he tried to talk about the issue, she didn't want to discuss it because it hurt even more. He knew she felt like she'd failed him, but that couldn't be further from the truth. He didn't know what else to do, but one thing was for sure—he didn't want her to know that he too was miserable.

It was Christmastime, and ordinarily, that was a joyful time of the year. Usually Audrey's favorite. She made sure to make a big deal about buying presents and decorating. She baked her ass off and made a huge show of some damn elf that sat on a shelf for their daughter, Penelope. Tate didn't see the point in the stupid elf, but Audrey and Penelope loved her. Because of that, he went along with the games the elf played.

Honestly though, his heart didn't stand a chance when he looked into his baby girl's crystal blue eyes or even her momma's caramel eyes. They were his world and they were enough. He had told Audrey this many times, but she couldn't accept it. She wanted to give him more children, but unfortunately, they hadn't been lucky with the whole conceiving thing after they lost the last baby she was pregnant with. He still could hear her cries and it truly killed him. Since then, he hadn't been able to get her pregnant. She blamed herself, but sometimes, he felt as if it was his fault. He should be able to get a woman pregnant, and he had, twice, but they only had one blessing to show for it. Again, that was enough. He just wished Audrey would realize that.

Leaning back in his locker, he let out a long breath before running his fingers through his too long blond hair. He needed a haircut, but he wasn't worried about it. On top of worrying about the mental state of his beautiful wife, the holidays were always hard on him. Christmas had always been his family's favorite time of the year, and knowing they weren't here to watch Penelope grow almost brought tears to his eyes.

He wished he could shake off all the bad thoughts; he shouldn't be thinking them, not with Christmas so close, but he couldn't help it. He missed his family and he wanted his wife to be happy. He just wished it would all go away. He didn't want to be depressed on Christmas, not with how much it meant to Penelope.

"You're quiet. You okay?" Lucas, his best friend and his wife's brother-in-law, asked.

He nodded. "Just thinking. Holidays are hard."

Lucas moved a towel through his hair before looking over at him. "Yeah," he said with a nod. "How's Audrey holding up? Fallon thinks she is lying out her ass half the damn time."

"Yeah, she is," he confirmed, letting out a long breath. "I don't know what to do, honestly."

"How's the surrogate thingy going?" he asked, but Tate was already shaking his head.

"It isn't. She can't find someone she trusts. It's insane; I mean, surely they'll take care of the baby."

"Yeah, I mean, it worked for Harper."

"I told her this but she just doesn't want to pick someone. So I said, let's do the in vitro. I mean, we've already done the drugs and they've taken my sperm and her eggs. All they need is to go through with the procedure, but she is scared that it will be a waste of time because they say her uterus is weak. I'm telling you, she wants a baby so fucking bad. And sure, I would love another one, but I don't want this stress. I just want us to be happy. We have a beautiful daughter. What else do we need?"

Lucas slowly nodded and Tate felt desperate. Lucas didn't understand any of this. He was blessed with four gorgeous kids and a wife who wasn't driving him crazy now that she wasn't pregnant. Audrey was great pregnant, horny as hell and drove him mad with her need for him, so he wouldn't mind doing nine months of that again. But above all, he just wanted her to have everything she wanted. "I just want her to be happy, and I'll do anything to get her there."

"I know, buddy. You're really good to her."

Lucas cupped his shoulder as Tate said, "Because I love her. More than anything, and no matter how many times I tell her that, she doesn't listen."

"She is hardheaded like her sister. It will work out."

Tate didn't think it would, but he nodded and agreed, "I hope so."

After getting to the hotel later that night, he set his computer up and Skyped Audrey. Waiting for her to answer, he leaned back in his bed and grinned when his beautiful daughter's face filled the screen. Her dusty brown hair was in curls down her shoulders, her eyes bright as she waved wildly at him.

"Daddy!"

He sat up, waving back at her. "Hello, my sweetheart. How's Daddy's girl?"

Her grin was unstoppable as she said, "Good! I made cupcakes today at the shop, and I'm bringing them to class tomorrow."

"Wonderful, where is Mommy?"

"Right here," Audrey said, coming into view. Her hair was in a messy bun, her eyes not as bright as he liked, and she wasn't really smiling. It wasn't the kind of smile he loved; it was a forced one.

"Hey, baby. I miss you two."

"We miss you!" Penelope yelled, throwing her arms up in the air.

"We do," Audrey agreed, her eyes lighting up a little bit. "Great game. We love watching you win, huh, Pennyloo?"

Penelope nodded quickly. "You're so awesome, Daddy."

That warmed his heart, but as he eyed his wife, he couldn't shake the feeling that she had been crying. "Thank you, baby. You are too."

"Duh! I'm Mommy's baby!"

Audrey grinned at that, kissing Penelope's temple before looking back at the camera.

"There is my true smile. I miss seeing it," he admitted and Audrey looked down.

"Yeah, I need to smile more, huh?"

"Yeah!" Penelope agreed. "I love when you're happy."

"Me too," Tate said as Audrey met his gaze.

"I'll be happy once you're home again," she said, and he knew that wasn't the truth. "Tell Daddy goodnight and that you love him. It's time for bed. I let her stay up to talk to you. She missed you today, huh, sweetheart?"

Penelope nodded quickly as Tate said, "I miss you too, sweetheart. I'll be home in two more sleeps."

"I can't wait!" she cheered.

"Me too," Audrey said with a grin on her face, and he smiled back.

"I love you, Pennyloo, and I miss you," he said and Penelope giggled.

"I miss you, Daddy! I love you so so so so so so so so so so so so so," she took in a deep breath and continued, "So so so so so so so so MUCH!!"

He grinned widely at her before kissing the camera. "I miss you more than that and then some. Now goodnight, sweetheart."

"Night, Daddy," she said before kissing the camera and then Audrey.

"I'll be up in a few minutes, okay? Tuck in all your dolls," she said and Tate chuckled.

Bedtime was a long, drawn-out process in the Odder household. It took Penelope at least ten minutes to tuck in all her dolls and then another ten minutes of a story before either Audrey or he had to lie with her, talking about their day. She hated to sleep and they didn't mind catering to her needs. The perks of being the princess in the house.

Once Penelope hopped away, Audrey looked at the screen and tried to smile. "I figure when you get home, we'll decorate. Christmas is right around the corner."

He nodded. They had three weeks, but it was coming up quick. "Yeah, usually we are set up after Thanksgiving."

She shrugged. "Yeah. Just haven't been in the mood."

"Yeah," he agreed, and then he decided he didn't like this. "Audrey," he said since she was looking down, picking at her nails.

She glanced up. "Yeah?"

He was tired of it all. If she wouldn't do what needed to be done, he was going to do it. He was going to make her happy.

"Make an appointment."

"Huh?" she asked, perplexed.

"Make an appointment for the in vitro. You want a baby; then we'll get one."

"Okay," she answered and his brows came up.

That was entirely too easy.

"What?"

She smiled. "I already made the appointment yesterday. I just didn't know if I should tell you because what if it doesn't stick?"

His brows came together. "So you weren't going to tell me?"

She shook her head. "I've already disappointed you enough."

Letting out a long breath, he swore he was going to have words with his wife. "I am going to shake you, woman."

She smiled. "Oh really?"

"Yes," he said with a nod but without conviction. He wouldn't lay a hand on her, but he wanted her to know he was annoyed. "You've not, in any way, disappointed me, my love. You have been a perfect wife. Great lover and the best mother imaginable."

Her lips curved as she shook her head. "I've only given you one baby."

"And she is enough, Audrey, honestly. You have made my life twenty times better. I was lost without you. So please, don't ever say anything like that again, and also don't hide things from me. I don't like that."

"I just want to make you happy," she said, her eyes clouding with tears. He wanted to be there; he wanted to hold her and reassure her.

Clearing his throat, he smiled. "Audrey, baby, just looking at you makes me happy. You are my everything, baby."

She smiled as she nodded. "You're mine."

"Good, now when is the appointment?"

"Tomorrow."

"I'll be there."

"You have a game."

"I'll fly in and fly back out. What time?"

"Eight thirty. Piper is getting Pennyloo and taking her to school since Fallon just had Emery and all."

He nodded and then promised, "I'll be there."

Her face lit up. "That would be awesome. I'm scared."

"Don't be," he said with a crooked grin. "I'll be right beside you."

"I love you," she said, and as he watched a tear slowly roll down her face, his heart broke a little bit in his chest.

"I love you, baby," he promised and he always would. "And, babe?"

"Yeah?"

"It's going to work. I can feel it in my bones."

Another tear fell as she nodded. "I hope so."

"It will," he promised. "And what you want will be in your belly instead of under the tree."

She let out a sob as she nodded, and he knew in his heart that this was going to work. It had to.

It just did.

All Audrey wanted for Christmas was to get pregnant.

It was actually on her list of things she wanted for Christmas. It also included a new pair of Louis Vuitton heels and maybe a purse. Oh, and she would really like a locket from Tiffany's with Tate and Penelope's picture in it. It was a short list, but at the top was having a baby. Which was really a gift for Tate.

He constantly reminded her that Penelope and she were enough, but she could see it in his eyes. He wanted what everyone else had and that was a lot of damn kids. She wanted that too. She had always wanted kids, but when she learned she couldn't have them, she let it go. But then she got pregnant by the grace of God, and for the last five years, all she'd wanted was for it to happen again.

Not saying that Penelope wasn't her world, because she was. Her sweet baby was everything she could ever have wished for. She was her mini me, but Audrey really did want to have another. Just one more. She wanted a sibling for Penelope. Maybe a sister like she had or even a brother. She didn't care. She just wanted someone for Penelope to grow up with, but most of all, she wanted to be a complete woman.

Someone who could provide Tate with everything he wanted.

"You're shaking," he informed her, kissing her temple. She was lying on her back, her legs up in stirrups, waiting for the longest thirty minutes of her life to end. The doctor had just inserted the embryos into her, and she was praying to God one of them stuck. She'd had spent many sleepless nights researching this process and had driven herself mad with worry, but she had to believe in this for it to work. She had been sad for far too long, and if it didn't work, then she would pick a surrogate.

They would have a baby.

Or maybe they would adopt?

She wasn't sure, but she hoped this worked.

"Please, let this work," she whispered to herself, but Tate was there, his arm wrapped around the top of her head, rubbing her jaw as his lips dusted her cheek.

"It will," he whispered back, kissing her again, the hair on his jaw tickling her.

She closed her eyes as she sucked in a deep breath.

It would work.

Two weeks later, Audrey wasn't so sure.

She just felt off. She was cramping and she was sure that she was miscarrying all of the babies they put in her. She wasn't sure, but her hopes were down in the dumps. Not even seeing her precious, sweet daughter make cupcakes had lightened the mood. They had made Christmas cupcakes to take to the hospital Tate was volunteering at that afternoon. She loved when he did this, and she was even more excited that she and Penelope got to go. They were going to spoil the "sick babies," as Penelope called them, and Audrey loved how excited her daughter was about going. But even standing there, watching as Tate and Penelope read to a couple little girls, she couldn't smile.

Tomorrow was her appointment where they would do a blood test to see if she was pregnant. She kept telling herself she was, but it just didn't seem real. Why was she cramping and hurting so bad? Some people said they experienced the same, but it wasn't that common. She was going to make herself sick with worry, and what good would that do?

As she let out a long breath, Piper leaned into her and smiled.

"Stop."

Audrey shook her head. She loved her best friend, but even right now, Piper couldn't make her feel better. She wouldn't feel better until she knew one way or another.

"It's going to be fine," Piper reassured.

"And what if it isn't?"

"Then you try again, or you adopt, try a surrogate. There are other options."

"I want to carry my own child," she whispered, tears stinging her eyes. "I want to be the wife Tate deserves."

"You are," Piper said, squeezing her arm. "And I know for a fact he has told you that. So stop this. Be happy you have a healthy husband and daughter because some people don't even get that."

"I know, but—"

Lifting her daughter, Katarina, up on her hip, Piper shook her head. "No, no but, you've been doing this for far too long. Look around, Audrey. These people are fighting for their children, begging the good Lord above to save them so they can keep loving them, and you have it all. You have a loving husband, a gorgeous daughter, and they are healthy. What else do you really need? You're being selfish and hurting yourself. The stress and the depression are going to have you pushing up daisies, and then Tate and Pennyloo will be alone. Do you want that?"

Audrey swallowed hard as she blinked back the tears. Her heart hurt because Piper was right. She was being selfish. She had everything she could ever want. A successful business, family that loved her, and like Piper said, a husband and daughter who thought she hung the moon and the stars. She was blessed. To the extreme. And maybe instead of wanting more, she should be grateful for what she had. She wasn't even supposed to have been able to have kids, and she'd been convinced she would never find a man to love her because of it, but Tate loved her without children. He loved her no matter what.

So why was she making such a huge deal about this?

Disgusted in herself, she looked around the room at all the families who watched as their children tried to enjoy the day. It brought tears to her eyes. She had spent so much time worrying about having babies when these people were struggling to keep theirs. Swallowing past the lump in her throat, she took in a deep breath and let her shoulders fall.

"No, I don't."

"I know," Piper agreed. "So stop. If tomorrow you're not pregnant, then that is God's will and let it go. You have it all, and you're awesome on top of that."

Audrey smiled as she blinked back her tears, nodding her head. When she looked up, Tate was looking back at her, his eyes intensely on hers, and she smiled. A real smile. Just for him. He loved her, and boy, did she love him. He was everything a woman could hope for, and he did everything in his power to make her happy. She wanted to do the same, and she thought that was having a baby, but maybe it wasn't. Maybe it was just loving him that would make him happy. He had told her that, and if she got her head out of her ass, maybe she would start to listen.

Standing up to his full six foot seven glory, he closed the distance between them and wrapped his arms around her, kissing her temple. "Thinking hard?" he whispered before placing a small kiss to her head again.

She smiled, lacing her fingers around his thin frame. "Just thinking about tomorrow."

"Not stressing, right?"

She shook her head. "Not anymore. I've decided that if I'm not, then I'm done. We have everything we need."

"You're right, and I've told you this a billion times."

She smiled at his statement as she ran her fingers down his jaw. "I'm sorry I've been a crazy lunatic for the last four years. I should have listened to you sooner. I should have realized I have everything I need with just you two."

He cupped her face, his eyes boring into hers as a smile pulled at his lips. "I know how you are. You want to please and make everyone happy. You've driven me insane—I'm not going to lie—but I love you. So it's okay. I'll take the crazy any time of the day as long as I get to kiss you whenever I please."

She grinned as her arms went around him, running her nose along the bottom of his jaw. "Like now?"

"Yeah," he said with a grin. "Now is great."

When he dropped his mouth to hers, she closed her eyes and lost herself in his kiss. His lips were always so soft and inviting and hit her straight in the gut. When a little body came between them, Audrey pulled away, smiling as she looked down to find her daughter watching them. Her eyes, blue like the ocean, were wide as she looked up at them, her arms tightening around Audrey's leg.

"Mommy, is it cupcake time?"

Audrey nodded. "It is! Let's eat."

Kissing Tate's jaw, she went to step away, but he stopped her, his fingers lacing with hers as his eyes met hers. "Tomorrow though, you'll get your Christmas wish."

She smiled. "Santa came five years ago and gave me you and our daughter. There isn't anything else on my list."

He laughed. "Liar, I know you want those shoes."

"Oh yes, those shoes I do need."

Wrapping his arms around her, he chuckled before kissing her cheek, and then they were off to hand out cupcakes. As they spent the rest of the afternoon at the hospital, she would have been lying if she'd said she hadn't thought of the following day. But instead of the feeling of dread and nervousness in her belly, she pushed to be positive. She wasn't going to stress anymore. She wasn't going to worry. If it happened, then she would be elated. If it didn't, then she would accept that and move on.

She had everything she needed.

But as she sat in the chair the next day, a needle in one arm and her other hand clutching Tate's, her stomach was back to knots. She tried so hard to be positive, but her emotions were everywhere. She wanted to be excited for the possibility, but she also wanted to be realistic. This probably wasn't going to happen. Also, her pregnancy test was faint—not a no, but not a yes—and that was a disappointment. She had read that when people were pregnant, their tests were bright and happy, but hers wasn't sure. It was as if her body wasn't sure if it wanted to be pregnant or not.

"We'll know in a couple hours. Why don't y'all go to lunch?" the nurse suggested, and Audrey nodded as she looked over at Tate.

"Sounds like a plan," he agreed, and soon they were at the closest steakhouse. They ate in silence. Well, Tate ate; Audrey picked at her salad.

"I thought we said we weren't going to stress?"

She let out a breath as she nodded. "I'm not stressing, really. It's more I'm nervous."

He took her hand and kissed her knuckles. "Don't. Either way, we are happy. Right?"

She laced her fingers with his and looked deep in his eyes. She could see her whole future in his eyes. The two of them raising Pennyloo, going on trips, watching Daddy win, and building Audrey Jane's into something that maybe Penny would want. Even though Audrey was pretty sure her baby was going to grow up to help people. Maybe as a doctor or a missionary. They would send her to college, and one day Tate would walk her down the aisle. It was all there, and the whole time she would be completely and entirely in love with him.

"Right," she agreed. "I love you, Tate Oooooodder."

He smiled at his nickname from her and leaned across the table, his lips only a breath away. "And I love you a hell of a lot more than that, Mrs. Oooooodder."

As he pressed his lips to hers, Audrey's eyes fell shut as her mouth moved with his. She felt completely whole. As if nothing else could touch her.

That was, until her phone rang.

Slowly they parted and looked down at her phone to see that it was the doctor. Sucking in a deep breath, she looked at Tate but he was staring at the phone. Reaching for it, his hand still cupping her face, he hit answer and then the speaker button.

Looking at her, he said, "Hello?"

"Can I please speak with Audrey Odder?"

"This is she," she said breathlessly, and Tate moved his thumb along her jaw soothingly.

"Oh, hey! Okay, so your levels are well past five hundred! You're pregnant!"

Tears were streaming down her face before the doctor even finished talking. Her heart felt as if it was pounding so hard it was going to break her ribs. She felt as if she were flying or dreaming. Was this really happening?

"Really?"

"Yes! Congratulations!"

A sob left her lips as she covered her face, crying into her hands. She was pregnant. She was going to have a baby. Tate's baby. Dropping her hands, she looked across the table and met Tate's tearful gaze.

"We are having a baby."

Dropping the phone, Tate pushed the chair back and came around, pulling her out of her chair. Wrapping his arms tightly around her, he kissed her hard as he picked her up off the ground, holding her as his mouth moved with hers. Pulling back, his eyes bored into hers as his lips curved in the biggest smile she had ever seen. She knew her smile was probably bigger.

She had prayed and wished for a baby for the last four Christmases, and finally, she was pregnant. She decided she didn't need anything else on that list because she was loved by the two most amazing people in the world and was also pregnant.

What more could she ever want?

Piper & ERIK

"Audrey is pregnant!"

Erik Titov looked over at his wife and smiled. She looked gorgeous, as always. Wearing black tights with a long purple sweater, her dirty-blond hair was down along her shoulders, her makeup done nicely, while her purple lipstick shone on her lips. She looked delectable, and he couldn't wait to get her home. Yeah, his family was in town, but surely they wouldn't hear too much.

They were on their way to his benefit where they would give over one hundred disadvantaged kids hockey equipment and Christmas presents. It was one of his favorite benefits, and he was excited to see the faces of the kids as they opened all the things that he and Piper had personally picked out for each of them. Hearing that his best bud and his wife were expecting, though, took his excitement up another level.

"Really?"

"Yup!" she basically cheered as she typed wildly on her phone. "She is nervous she might miscarry, but surely she'll be good, right?"

He nodded. "Let's hope so. They both want this really bad."

"They do," she said with a nod. "Even though yesterday we were talking, and I told her she was being selfish. I was worried she would be mad, but she wasn't. Thank God. I really need to get a filter sometimes."

"I love your no-filter ass."

She smacked him playfully as they pulled into the arena. Shutting the car off, he got out and helped her out before slamming her door, pulling her into the crook of his arm.

"You look hot tonight," he told her, giving her an exaggerated wink. "I think I need you to put out when we get home."

She giggled, wrapping her arms around his waist. "With your mom and dad at the house? Please."

"We've done it before."

Her face turned red, and he knew it wasn't from the cold. "Maybe."

"No maybe about it," he decided. "I'm going to do you against their door."

She gasped. "You wouldn't dare!"

"You wouldn't stop me," he challenged back.

Her grin told him everything he needed to know. She wouldn't. And when she said that, his body went hot. His wife was still too hot to trot and drove him absolutely mad with lust. It was hard to stay off her most of the time, but she did have a job. And he did have to play hockey. Also, both of them had to be parents. He was pretty sure that Dimitri and Katarina wouldn't want to see Mommy and Daddy having sex every five seconds. No matter how badly they wanted each other.

Kissing her temple, he closed his eyes and took in her scent. When he held her like this, cherishing her, he couldn't help but think how he'd almost pushed her away. How he almost didn't have everything he hadn't known he needed, and when he thought about that, he hated himself. But then she would look up at him, her crystal blue eyes shining, her lips curved in such a sinful way, and he knew that she loved him. With her whole soul. And he loved her just as much, if not more.

"I love you, Piper."

She grinned, moving her fingers through the hair on his jaw. "I love you too. Come on, it's cold as hell."

He chuckled as he reached for the door and headed inside. Once inside, the many kids greeted them and the festivities started. They had catered some BBQ, and Audrey had supplied the cupcakes along with a huge cake shaped like a hockey stick. When it was time for all the kids to get new equipment, Erik was swallowing back his tears. Moms were crying, kids were bursting at the seams with excitement, and wrapping paper was flying everywhere. He always cherished it when someone told him thank you or when they made a huge deal about something they'd gotten them.

He didn't have it easy growing up. It was hard, especially after his brother, Jakob, left home. Instead of presents, he got his ass beat. Instead of a big holiday dinner, he usually ate Spam and crackers. It was hell, but he knew because of it, he was the man he was now. A good man who loved his wife and kids more than anything in the world and made sure they all knew that. But he would have time to spoil his family on Christmas.

It was time to spoil his hockey kiddos now.

When they all started opening the gifts that he and Piper had picked out, their faces were priceless and something he would always hold near to his heart.

Knowing that he brought some light to a kid's Christmas when their home life wasn't good was really the true meaning of the holiday.

With Dimitri and Katarina in their stroller, Erik pushed the kids through the Green Hills mall in search of Tiffany's. He hated shopping, but they had to get something for Piper for Christmas. He was leaving in a few days for a short road trip before Christmas, and he wanted to make sure the kids got to help him pick something out. Getting rid of Piper and his parents was a feat, but he managed it. Now if Dimitri could stop throwing his sippy cup out of the stroller and Katarina could stop crying, life would be grand.

Stopping in front of a glass case, he could see that the girl behind the desk couldn't agree more.

"Sir, can I help you?"

Erik nodded. "Yeah, I need a mom ring," he barked as he hauled Katarina up into his arms. The wiggly one-year-old didn't want to be held though and promptly smacked him in the head. "No, that's not nice."

"Not nice!" Dimitri yelled and Erik rolled his eyes. The kid was his own personal parrot. He copied anything and everything Erik said, and usually that got him in trouble.

Katarina's little lip quivered, and then she wailed at the top of her lungs. Trying to soothe her, he looked back at the salesgirl and said, "Mom ring, August birthday and a July birthday."

"Platinum, white gold, or gold?"

"Platinum, big stones, diamonds, and the prettiest you got."

"Prettiest you got," Dimitri said.

"Price limit?"

"There isn't one," he said, and when she smiled, he shot her one back.

Then Dimitri added, "There isn't one."

The girl gave Dimitri a sweet smile before walking away and Erik shook his head.

"You need to cut that out."

"Cut it out."

"No, you cut it out."

"No, you cut it out."

"You're copying me."

"You're copying me!" he cheered before grinning extra big. Erik shook his head in disbelief just as Katarina dumped her drink down the front of his jacket.

"Lovely, my love."

"My love!" was Dimitri's comment, while Erik's sweet baby shot him a little grin.

Chuckling, he decided it was lovely. She was his princess and Dimitri was his little dude. They both drove him insane, but they were his. Just as Piper was his too. Erik kissed Katarina's cheek, and she cuddled into his neck as the girl brought back a few rings.

"Here you go, we can have it all ordered and ready before Christmas."

Erik nodded, satisfied since he was worried he might be too late. "Awesome. Okay, guys, which one?"

Dimitri stood in his stroller and peered over the counter. He then exclaimed, "That one, Daddy!"

Erik was almost tempted to copy him since that's what Piper did to make him stop, but they weren't at home. Looking at the ring, he decided that was the one. The two stones would make a heart with three diamonds around it that would represent Erik and the kids. It was perfect and he knew she would love it.

"That's it."

Piper Titov's head fell to the side as she took in the elaborate Dr. Seuss mural she was doing for her nephew Journey's room. The little bugger loved Dr. Seuss, and while she had done his hockey mural only a couple years ago, she was happy to change it to make her little guy happy. She was sure her niece Ally was next, but for the time being, she was going to make the best Dr. Seuss mural in the world.

Not only was the famous cat causing havoc on the wall but he was joined by Thing One and Thing Two, along with Sam, the Lorax, and many other timeless characters from the wonderful books. This was probably her favorite mural yet. Smiling, she moved her brush along the wall, the color vibrant as she let out a contented sigh. She loved her life. She had the hottest husband imaginable, two superawesome kids, and family and friends people begged for.

But.

And she hated that there was a but.

But.

She was getting bored painting murals.

She knew it was crazy, and she knew that she was making a killing doing them, but she was getting bored! She had been doing this for almost four years and she was kinda done. She needed more of a challenge and found that in book cover design. She hadn't told anyone yet, but for the last three months, she had been designing covers for her author friends. It was so exhilarating! Bringing a book to life was becoming something she had to do. Something she was born to do. She loved reading, and being able to sum up the book with a simple image gave her a crazy rush. The only problem was she had made a huge deal saying that painting murals was her life.

She knew people expected her to change her mind, but she wanted to stick with something. Unfortunately, she just wasn't happy doing it anymore, and she wasn't sure what she should do. It was Christmastime, not really the ideal time to tell her husband she wanted to change careers. Erik didn't care about the money since he made enough for their family and then some, but she wanted to contribute. She didn't make as much money doing covers as she did doing the murals. Would she feel like a contributing part of the family? And plus, what would everyone think?

They'd probably roll their eyes and think of her as flighty again. It was a depressing thought because she didn't want to be flighty. She wanted to be strong, know what she wanted, but she just got bored with the same thing all the time.

Being a mother and wife was the only thing she didn't get bored with. It was everything she had ever thought it would be, and sometimes she couldn't believe she had been so scared to have Dimitri. He honestly brought out the best in her. He also helped his daddy get his head out of his ass and love her, so really, he was the biggest blessing in her life. As well as Katarina. She was so full of life and so perfect. She drove them all crazy since she was sort of a crybaby, but Piper loved her so damn much. They had the perfect little family, and she couldn't wait for the future.

"Wow, looks amazing."

Piper looked over her shoulder and smiled as her older sister Harper entered the room.

"Thanks," she said with a grin as she dipped her brush in the paint. "Where did you go? I got here expecting some food, but only Jakob was here with the kids, and no food was provided. When I asked where you were, Jakob wouldn't tell me."

She laughed but it was more of a shocked laugh, not a ha-ha funny one. "Funny story, actually."

Piper's brows came up. "What's up?"

"We are getting an extra special Christmas present this year."

Still confused, Piper asked, "Huh? What?"

Shaking her head, Harper met Piper's gaze and said, "I'm pregnant."

Confused, Piper's head tilted to the side. "But you couldn't get pregnant."

"I know."

"And your tubes are tied."

"I know. I'm ten weeks and had no clue."

"Huh?" Piper asked, completely shocked. "Ten weeks!"

"Yeah, I'm as shocked as you are. Believe me. We both are. I haven't had my period, but it been spotty since the tubal anyway. But I haven't been sick or anything. The only reason I went in was because my tits have been hurting so bad, I thought I had cancer or something. Nope, a baby."

Piper laughed. "Wow. That's so awesome! Congrats!"

Wrapping her sister in a half hug, she found that her eyes were clouding with tears. Harper had wanted another baby so badly after Ally. She'd even asked Piper and her twin, Reese, to carry it for her, but then they found a surrogate and had Journey. Now though, she was going to carry her own child.

"Audrey's pregnant too! This is so awesome."

Harper laughed. "All us Assassins women are always pregnant together. Damn hockey players are fertile as hell."

"No shit, right? That's so cool! I am so excited for you," Piper said, squeezing her again, and when she pulled back, her sister had big fat tears rolling down her face. She could see the excitement in Harper's eyes and couldn't be happier.

"I'm nervous I could lose it again, but I mean, I'm ten weeks. I think God did it that way so I wouldn't stress and worry, you know?"

Tears flooded Piper's eyes as she wiped away her sister's. "Yeah, this one is going to stick and stay. It has to—it went through tied tubes to get here!"

"I just can't believe it!"

"Me either! It's freaking amazing. Come here!"

Harper laughed and wrapped her arms tightly around Piper as she sobbed into her shoulder. Piper loved Christmastime; it was the best time for miracles.

And Harper's and Audrey's babies were just that.

After finishing for the day and loving on Harper and her family, Piper went home to her own family. As she drove, a huge grin was on her face. Her sister was pregnant. What a freaking miracle. When her phone started to ring, she reached for it to see that it was her twin.

"Hey!"

"Have you talked to Harper?" Reese basically yelled with excitement.

"I did! Can you believe it?"

"No! Oh my God, really, Piper, I've been sitting here crying, I am so happy for her."

"Me too, I cried. I just can't believe it."

"It's a damn miracle, I tell you!"

"I know. It's so awesome," Piper agreed. "Next is you, lady."

"Oh, hell no! You're next."

"Whatever, we are done. We have two, a boy and girl, what more do we need?"

"I have a handful of a son and then a niece who is getting married. I'm too broke to have any more."

Piper laughed. "Liar. You can afford ten more."

She scoffed. "Claire is going to make us broke. You know she wants to pay for everyone to fly in? Phillip told her to kiss his ass, and I'm like, Claire, you haven't even picked a date!"

Piper's grin grew. Her niece was going to drive Phillip and Reese insane with her wedding.

"I swear, he is going to be gray before this wedding happens. My poor husband."

"He'll be fine. It's awesome. Claire and Jude love each other so much."

"Yeah, I know. She is so happy, and I love when she is happy. I just wish she'd wait at least another ten years."

Piper scoffed. "Please, in ten years, she'll have kids and stuff."

"Oh, Lord help us all. Could you imagine her raising kids in Vegas? The horror," she said and Piper couldn't help but laugh.

"Jeez, Reese, you sound like Grandma!"

"Shut up!" she yelled, and Piper couldn't stop her laughter if she tried. "I was just calling because of Harper and then to ask what time Christmas dinner is."

"Mom said four and presents after."

"Okay cool, just making sure. I'll talk to you later."

"All right, love you."

"Love you," Reese said just as Piper pulled into her garage. Shutting the car off, she locked everything up and shut the garage door before heading inside. Within seconds, she was attacked by two little people before her husband wrapped her in a hug, kissing her lips.

"Well, what a greeting," she said, breathless, as he parted, kissing her nose.

"We missed you," he said. "And they are driving me insane."

She giggled as she picked up Katarina. Usually, she took the kids with her to her murals, but since Erik was home, they'd stayed with him.

"They tend to do that. Hey, Alla and Cooper!" she said to her in-laws. They were staying for a couple weeks for Christmas and she loved having them.

"Hey, honey, dinner is almost done," Alla said as Cooper sent her a grin.

"Awesome. Hey, have y'all talked to Jakob today?"

All three of them shook their heads, and Piper decided that she would allow him to share the happy news. Alla and Cooper had been hinting for another grandchild. They weren't going to get it from Erik and Piper. They were done.

"Why?" Erik asked.

"No reason," she said, putting Katarina down and walking past them to change and shower. Like she knew he would, Erik followed her and shut the door behind them.

"What are you doing?" she asked, buying time.

"Following you," he said before sliding his hands down her thighs, pressing his growing erection against her ass. "I love you," he whispered in her ear, kissing the spot below it.

"I love you," she said, turning in his arms and pressing her lips to his. When she pulled back though, he didn't let her get far before he deepened the kiss, his hands sliding into the pockets of her jeans. Closing her eyes, she got lost in his kiss and didn't realize he was walking her backward to the bed until he was lying on top of her, his hands going up into her shirt.

Grinning, she pulled away. "Erik, our children and your parents are in the room over. They got an earful the other night. Come on," she pleaded as her eyes rolled into the back of her head. He had found her nipple, and he knew that was her hot spot. Gasping, her fingers tangled in his hair, but then banging started at the door, followed by Katarina wailing, "Mommy!"

Letting her nipple go, he kissed the spot between her breasts and grinned. "Your kid is a cockblock."

She giggled at that before pushing him off her and going to open the door to her special little people. "What do you need, love bug?"

"You," she decided before throwing her arms up. Dimitri came running in and jumped on the bed on top of Erik, hitting him right in the groin. As Piper laughed, Erik wallowed in pain while Dimitri just grinned.

"Ugh! You broke my balls, kid!" he groaned and Piper shook her head as Katarina giggled.

"I broke Daddy's balls," Dimitri said with a huge grin. "He gonna be okay?"

"Yeah, he's fine," she said, sitting down and patting Erik's butt. Wrapping her arm around Dimitri, she asked, "What did you do with Daddy today?"

"We bought you a ring for Christmas."

"Dimitri! You weren't supposed to tell her!" Erik scolded, but Dimitri didn't seem to care. "I told him not to tell you."

"He doesn't listen," Piper laughed. "Is it pretty?"

"Oh yeah, so pretty. Give it to her, Daddy!"

"No! It's for Christmas, and it isn't even done yet!"

Piper giggled some more as Katarina wiggled out of her lap and then out the door. Dimitri followed right along behind her, leaving Piper alone with her husband. They came, took her loving, and then were gone. That's how it was in the Titov house.

Sending him a wide grin, she asked, "New ring, huh?"

He shrugged. "Maybe. I might go change it."

She lay back in the bed, cuddling into his side before kissing his jaw. "I can't wait to open it."

"Yeah, well, it's ruined," he complained and she shook her head.

"Never. I'll be surprised and thankful. Don't worry."

"Good," he said, wrapping his arms around her and kissing her nose. Looking deep into her eyes, he smiled and she felt breathless. He loved her. So damn much and she knew he would no matter what.

"I don't want to paint murals anymore."

Wow. Did she just blurt that out?

His brows came together. "That's outta left field."

She nodded. "Yeah."

"Why not?"

"I don't know. I haven't told you, but I've been designing book covers for the last three months. I love it."

She could see the shock in his eyes, but then a knowing grin came over his lips as he nodded. "That's cool. Bored with the murals, already?"

She smiled sheepishly. "Yeah. Is that bad?"

"For you, no. I'm surprised you didn't get bored sooner."

"So you aren't mad?" she asked, hopeful.

"Fuck no, baby. You do what you want. I'll just be standing here, cheering you on. No matter what."

Her smirk grew as she cuddled deeper against him. "You are the best husband."

"I know," he agreed, a grin pulling at his lips. "And you're the best wife."

Christmas wasn't even here yet, and she knew he had a beautiful gift for her, but no matter what the season, her husband continually gave her the best gift of all.

And that was his love and ultimate support.

Reese & PHILLIP

Phillip Anderson was going to kill Jude Sinclair.

He didn't give two fucks if Claire loved him, or even if it was almost Christmas and his momma was going to be sad she lost one of her boys, Phillip was going to kill him.

He didn't know what it was about playing against the kid, but it brought out the asshole in both of them, and soon they were messing and chirping at each other through the whole game. For Phillip, it was the fact that Jude was defiling his niece, and because of that, he hated him. He wasn't sure what she saw in the little idiot, but she sure did love him. Enough to marry his punk ass. Phillip shuddered at the thought.

"Come on, old man! Can't keep up? I've already scored on you twice tonight."

Despite the fact that he had, Phillip glared.

"Shut up, you little shit," Phillip sneered as he waited for the puck to drop.

"Ignore him, Anderson," King hollered at him.

"He's a punk. Don't let him get to you," Titov agreed. "Play hockey, you fuck face, before you have the whole team kicking your ass."

"Bring it. I'd take all of you out," the cocky little shit said.

"You couldn't take out the trash. Shut the hell up and play hockey," Shea bellowed at him, and he cowered a bit, but Phillip didn't miss the defiance in his eyes. He couldn't fight him though; they were down by two because of his little ass, and they had to catch up. Ending up in the box wouldn't help the cause of winning, but this kid was dead set on driving Phillip insane.

Meeting Phillip's gaze, Jude said, "I was considering naming our first kid after you, but for that to happen, I'm going to need you to play some decent hockey."

Yeah. See the kid brought out some kind of rage inside of him, and without even realizing it, Phillip dropped his gloves and slammed his fist into Jude's nose. The crowd lost their marbles as the two duked it out. He took the punches like a champ and felt empowered when the kid started to look rattled. But when Jude slammed his fist into Phillip's jaw, it knocked him off-balance. Soon he was lying on his ass and the fight was stopped as the crowd again lost their shit cheering for their prize player.

Jude punk ass Sinclair.

Little asshole.

After being razzed by his teammates for getting knocked on his ass by his soon-to-be son-in-law—ugh, he shuddered again—Phillip decided he needed a stiff drink and headed down to the hotel bar. The hotel was decorated for the season, and usually that made him happy, but he was still pissed about Jude and the fact that, at any second, Claire would set a date and he'd have to give her away to that little shit.

He was surprised how much the upcoming wedding affected him. He should be happy for her; she loved this kid something crazy, but man, the thought that she wouldn't be his but that little shit's killed him inside. Phillip loved Claire more than an uncle ordinarily would, but that was because she was basically his. He was lucky to have such a beautiful, successful young lady as his niece—well, his daughter. He hadn't referred to her as his niece in a really long time. She was his daughter. His heart. And he wasn't about to hand that over to some little punk. Yeah, he'd agreed to it and had given Jude his blessing, but still it was a tough pill to swallow.

He'd hoped maybe she'd say no.

Taking a long pull of his drink, he groaned when his phone rang. He knew it was his wife, and while he wanted nothing more than to hear her voice, he knew he was about to get bitched out.

No reason to prolong the inevitable, he thought as he answered.

"Don't you think you're a little too old to be fighting? I mean, come on, he's a kid."

"A punk, had to shut him up," he informed her and smiled when she let out an annoyed breath. He loved driving her insane.

"Um, he knocked you on your ass. So really, who shut whom up?"

Phillip glared. "Are you my wife or his?"

"Oh hush, if you didn't go fighting our future son-in-law, then I wouldn't tease you."

"He had it coming."

"Well, I think it is just silly."

"Well, I think he is an asshole."

"He's the asshole marrying our baby, so I'm going to need you to suck it up and accept him."

His response was a grunt, but his smile was back when she laughed. Her laugh was so airy and happy; it always hit him straight in the core. He loved to make her laugh. And scream. "I miss you, woman."

"Aw, I miss you. Sawyer and I are making ornaments."

Disappointed, he said, "I thought you were going to wait for me."

"We are only doing the little ones. We'll do our family ones together."

"Oh, okay."

"I think I might wait till Claire gets in. She should be home in a couple days, even though for a minute there, I thought she wasn't coming."

Phillip panicked a bit. Everything had already changed so much; he needed Claire to come home for Christmas. "Huh? Why?"

"Jude has a game in New York."

"So?"

She scoffed. "Well, she wants to be with her fiancé."

"But we are her family."

"Phillip, come on," she deadpanned. "You can't blame her for wanting to be with him."

"Yes, I can," he said grumpily. "I don't like this."

"Really? I couldn't tell."

He glared even though she wasn't in front of him as she said, "She's coming home, he told her to, so she wouldn't miss Christmas with us since he was flying in and out. He won't even be able to see his family. They are going to do a late Christmas before New Year's. Apparently his momma isn't too happy, but she is dealing."

He knew he was being selfish, but he was glad that Claire was coming home. "She isn't happy about it, though?"

"Nope, not at all."

He kind of felt bad. He wanted her to be happy. So swallowing his pride, he said, "Did you tell her it was okay to go to New York?"

"Yeah, but Jude talked her out of it. He doesn't want her to miss Christmas with us."

He grunted again. "Guess I can't hate the kid that much, huh?"

"It would be nice if you didn't since very soon, he is going to be our son-in-law," she reminded him.

"Did she give you a date?" he asked quickly. "I haven't heard anything."

"Nope, but they are figuring it out. I think it's gonna be June."

"Ugh," he grunted again.

She giggled. "It's going to be great."

"It's going to be hell."

When the stool beside him was pulled out, he looked over to see Jude and instantly rolled his eyes. The only thing that pleased him was that his nose was swollen. At least he knew they wouldn't be getting married anytime soon.

"All right, let me call you back. The punk just sat next to me."

Reese laughed. "Be nice and tell him I said hi."

"Yeah, love you."

"Love you."

Hanging the phone up, he looked over again and said, "What do you want?"

"I was told I had to apologize to you. Apparently I am an instigator."

Phillip scoffed. "You think?"

Jude smirked as he shrugged. "I like harassing you."

"And I like hitting you," Phillip said, cheersing his drink to Jude before taking a long pull.

"Yeah, so, um…how about we bury the hatchet?"

"I'd rather chop you up with it," he said as cool as a cucumber, and Jude found that rather funny.

"Really, though," he said once his laughter subsided. "Claire doesn't want us fighting. We are getting married soon. You're going to be my father-in-law. I don't want us to be jerks to each other. We both love the same girl, you know?"

Not able to look at him, Phillip nodded. "Yeah."

"I'm going to love her till the day I die. I can promise you that. I won't ever hurt her."

He hated how the tears stung his eyes. He didn't want to trust this kid to do that because no one could love or protect her the way he could, but as he met the kid's gaze, he could see it in his eyes. Jude wasn't going to let anything happen to Claire, and Phillip knew that. That's why he'd given him his blessing to marry his special girl.

"I'll kill you if you break her heart."

He nodded. "I'll let you. I'm not going to do that."

"Good," he said with a nod. "Are you old enough to drink yet?"

Jude laughed. "Yeah."

"Let me buy you a drink then. We can shoot the shit before I'm ready to go to bed."

Jude nodded, a smile pulling at his lips. "I'd like that."

Phillip didn't like the idea of it at all, but he tried.

For Claire.

Running her fingers through her sweet boy's hair, Reese smiled as Sawyer drifted off to sleep. He had been fighting her lately, but it was only when Phillip was gone. Thankfully, she was patient and didn't mind sitting with him until he fell asleep. It was hard being without his daddy, she knew that, but when he woke up, Phillip would be home.

Thank God.

Her smile grew as Sawyer pursed his lips, his eyelashes kissing his cheeks as he dreamed about whatever the hell little boys dreamed of. Probably hockey, since he was Phillip's son. He looked so much like Phillip too, which helped when he was gone. She was so lucky to be his mommy and couldn't wait till Claire got home. Then their family would be complete again. At least for a little while before she had to go back home.

It had been hard living the last year without her, but they talked every day and it helped. Claire was her best friend and she hated being without her, but she wanted nothing more than for Claire to live her dreams. She was doing that, running the most successful burlesque club in Vegas, making a lot of money. She was amazing, and while it sucked for Reese as a mother, she couldn't be happier for Claire.

Kissing Sawyer's forehead, she slowly got out of bed and made it out of the room without a peep from her little man. So much had changed in the last couple years. She'd not only married the man of her dreams and helped raise a successful young lady, but she had a child of her own. Something she'd never thought would happen. Some days she wanted another one, but it made her nervous. Phillip, Claire, and Sawyer took all her love and then some. Could she love another one? She knew she could, but it was nerve-racking.

So much was happening. Claire was getting married, Harper was having a miracle baby, Piper would more than likely be changing careers at any moment, and then Reese's business was booming. Life was insane; did she really want to add another to that? Entering the kitchen, she poured herself a glass of tea before opening her computer to send out invoices to her dance moms. When the door opened though, she was surprised when she saw Phillip.

With a bright grin, she watched as he threw his bag down and headed for her. "You're home early."

"Yeah," he said simply before wrapping his arms around her. "I missed you."

She grinned as she kissed him deeply, his fingers playing with the hair at the nape of her neck. Pulling back, she rolled her eyes when she saw his blackened eye and the bruise along his jaw. He was so immature when it came to their future son-in-law.

"Where's my little man?"

"Sleeping."

"Good," he said before lifting her off her feet and onto the counter.

"What are you doing?" she giggled as he pulled down her dance shorts and panties with one swoop, throwing them to the ground.

"I'm hungry," he said simply before dropping his mouth to her core.

"Good God!" she gasped as he slid his tongue up her nether lips. Opening her up, he sucked her clit into his mouth, his fingers biting into her thighs as he devoured her with no cares in the world. Closing her eyes, she moved against his mouth, searching for her release. He drove her mad and she loved that he always wanted her. She used to worry that their need for each other would die out, but it still burned like the first moment she'd had the pleasure of having him in her. He was by far the hottest lover she had ever had, and she was more than happy that he was her last.

Coming off the counter, she came hard against his mouth, crying out his name as he continued to flick his tongue ruthlessly against her clit. Squeezing the edge of the counter, she cried out his name, trying to get away, but he wasn't letting her go. Sliding his finger inside her, he began to fuck her as she thrashed mindlessly underneath him.

"Fucking hell," she cried as her orgasm started to build again. Holding on, she took the mind-blowing pleasure he was causing, and when she rocketed off the counter against his talented mouth, his name falling from her lips, he pulled away and grinned down at her as she gasped for breath.

"You are the fucking hottest woman I have ever seen," he said as he took her by the hip, pulling her off the counter. Turning her around, he pushed her torso onto the counter and cracked his hand against her ass, causing her to cry out as her fingers held on to the counter. Closing her eyes, she gasped for breath as he entered her from behind, filling her completely. Lying against her, he kissed her shoulders as he slowly thrust inside of her. He was so big against her and she loved it. She loved how he completely took over when they made love. Sometimes, she surprised him and took control, but being fucked against the counter was just what she needed.

As he stood, taking her hips in his large hands, he pounded into her, their bodies slapping together in tune as he drove her completely out of her mind. She held on for dear life as he thrust once more and came, grunting before whispering her name. Stilling behind her, he moved his hand along her back then the curve of her ass before bringing her face to where he could kiss her.

Pulling away, he said, "I don't think I'll ever get enough of you."

She smiled. "I know I won't of you."

He kissed her again before backing away to clean up. She stood up and smiled as she watched his ass while he washed his hands. He was so hot. Thick and taut with mouthwatering muscles. When he glanced back at her, she said, "Welcome home."

He chuckled. "Thanks, babe."

Their gazes stayed locked for a long time, and then out of nowhere, and really, she didn't think she thought it through, she asked, "What do you think of trying for another baby?"

His brows came up before he chuckled. "You want another baby?"

She shrugged. "Maybe?" she said, unsure. Maybe he didn't want one.

"It's a yes or no question, Reese."

"Do you think it would be smart with Claire getting married and stuff?"

Coming to her, he wrapped his arms around her waist and looked deep in her eyes as he said, "I think if you want to have another baby, then let's do it."

Her heart exploded in her chest as she grinned. "Really?"

He nodded. "Yeah. I've wanted another kid for a while, but we all know how skittish you are," he teased, his grin growing. "I would love nothing more than to have another baby with you."

She begged her heart to be still, but that wasn't possible when she was locked in her husband's blue gaze. "I love you, Phillip Anderson."

He winked before cupping her face. "Well, Reese Anderson, you are very lucky because I love you so fucking much that it hurts. You complete me, baby, and I can't think of anything else I want in the world other than to be married and make babies with your sexy ass."

"Me either," she agreed before he dropped his mouth to hers. She would have kept kissing him if her phone hadn't rung. Parting, she looked down to see that it was Claire.

"It's our daughter."

"Answer it," he said, his hands falling to her bare ass. She really needed to put some pants back on before Sawyer woke up. Hitting answer, she put it on speaker as she said, "Hey, sweetheart."

"Hey! Whatcha doin'?" she asked, all happy and sweet.

Reese smiled as she slid her shorts back up and Phillip did the same. "Putting some pants on."

"Always good to have pants," Jude said and Reese's grin grew.

"Hey, Jude."

"Hey," he answered back, and she didn't miss the bored look on Phillip's face.

"Is Phillip home yet?" Claire asked.

"Yeah, I'm here. How are you, sweetheart?"

"Good! So glad you are there. We picked a date!"

Reese smiled when Phillip mouthed "fuck" before she said, "That's wonderful! When?"

"We want to do it Valentine's day!"

Phillip's eyes went wide as Reese's heart stopped. So soon? "Honey, that's in two months. There is no way we can find a venue."

"I called the mansion you guys got married at and someone canceled yesterday! They have opening, so I took it."

"Oh wow," she said, and she was convinced Phillip was having a heart attack.

"Are you sure, Claire? That's quick. Don't you want to wait, I don't know, ten years?" he asked.

Claire and Jude laughed, but Reese knew Phillip wasn't joking.

"Come on, Phillip, this is awesome! I hope you'll give me away. It would mean the world to me."

Yeah, that did him in, and Reese saw the tears in his eyes as he slowly nodded his head. "I would love to, Claire. I don't want to, but I will." Reese smiled as she leaned her head against his shoulder.

"Awesome! We are pretty excited."

"We are too. It's going to be amazing," Reese promised as she silently consoled her freaking out husband.

"Yeah, so merry Christmas to us, right? Finally got a day. It's the greatest gift, in my opinion, since agreeing about this has been a pain!"

Smiling, Reese laced her fingers with Phillip's and squeezed. She was pretty sure that he didn't agree about this being a great gift, but this was a part of life. They knew that Claire wasn't going to stay little forever, and they knew one day they would have to give her away. Jude was a good guy for that. He loved her and Reese trusted that he always would. While it didn't seem like it now, it was a great gift for them all. They were going to grow as a family with the possibility of a new child and then the reality of a new son-in-law.

And she was beyond thankful for that.

She had everything she'd never thought she needed.

As she kissed Phillip's jaw, he met her gaze and she said, "Merry Christmas to us all."

Leaning against the back wall, Claire Anderson surveyed her work with a wide smirk on her face. While three girls hung from chandeliers in seductive acrobatics, nine girls were on stage dancing provocatively to Sia's "Chandelier." It was her favorite dance she had choreographed yet. She was so proud of it, and it was everything she could have ever dreamed it could be. Moving her head to the music, she watched as her girls killed it. The crowd seemed to like it too. The place was packed, money flying as the men hooted and hollered at her girls.

She had done a fantastic job.

Content with everything, she smiled as the song ended and the girls went still, the lights going black. She knew this meant she had to go, but she didn't want to leave yet. She had seen the show over a billion times it seemed, but she couldn't get enough of it. This was her dream come true, and she loved watching it come to life. Watching until she knew she couldn't any longer, she said bye to everyone before rushing out of the club to the car that was waiting on her.

Sitting back in the seat, she let out a long breath before pulling her phone out. Clicking her fiancé's name, she smiled as she texted him.

Claire: I don't want to go home, I want to come to New York. I miss you.

She didn't have to wait long for his response.

Jude: I miss you, babe, but I'm gonna be so busy. Just enjoy your family. I'll meet you on Thursday. No biggie. I'll have your present and everything.

Claire: I don't want any, I want you.

Jude: I want you.

Claire: Then I am coming to New York.

Jude: Don't be difficult. You won't even miss me, you'll be too busy with Sawyer.

She would, but she really wanted to spend Christmas with the guy who made her life worth living. Yes, she loved Phillip, Reese, and Sawyer and really didn't want to spend the holiday without them, but she would if it meant she got to spend it with Jude. He had completely changed her life. He was the missing puzzle piece and gave her everything she needed. Yeah, she would see him the following day, but he wouldn't be there to open gifts and get stuffed on food on the actual day.

Christmas never really mattered to Claire before. That changed when she came to live with Phillip and even more when she got with Jude. He made everything twenty times better, and she knew that she would be sort of bummed that he wouldn't be there that morning. It sucked that he played and lived in a different state, but that's what they'd signed up for. They saw each other a lot and she got by, but she decided that she might not sign the next contract when hers was up. She wanted to be where Jude was, and because of that, she was saving money like crazy.

They might have to miss some holidays together for the next couple years, but when it was time to have kids, that wouldn't happen. She refused to raise kids in Vegas. And while it had been her hope and dream to headline a show, she figured that since she was doing it now, she wouldn't regret it when she quit to be a wife and mom. That would be a long time coming, but she knew what she wanted in life and that was Jude Sinclair.

Claire: Fine. I'm gonna be miserable without you.

Jude: I'm always miserable without you.

She smiled as his next text came in.

Jude: I'll see you soon. Have fun, get a dress or something for our wedding.

Her heart fluttered as she smiled dreamily. Their wedding. They were getting married very soon and she couldn't be happier. She couldn't wait to have Phillip give her away and to become Mrs. Jude Sinclair. When that happened, she'd have everything she could only dream of before.

Claire: 10-4 good buddy.

Jude: I love you. Have a safe flight.

Claire: I love you too. You too.

It was a long plane ride, but when she got off the plane and saw her aunt and nephew waiting for her, she almost came out of her skin in excitement. Running to them, she wrapped her arms around the both of them and hugged them tightly. It had been nine months since she had been home, and she couldn't believe how big Sawyer had gotten.

"My goodness! What are you feeding this kid? Miracle-Gro?"

Reese laughed as Claire took Sawyer, kissing him all over his sweet face. He tried to get away, but he wasn't going anywhere from his Claire. "He's Phillip's kid, what do you expect?"

Claire giggled as she nodded, hugging Sawyer tightly. "You have a point. He eats like a horse!"

"For sure! Ready? Your appointment is in an hour."

"Appointment?" she asked, confused.

"Yeah, Jude asked me to get you an appointment for wedding dress shopping!"

Claire's face broke out in a grin. "He did?"

"Yeah, he's kind of sweet."

"Yeah, he is," Claire agreed as they made their way to claim her baggage and then out into the freezing Tennessee air. It had been so long since she had been home that the cold surprised her, and she cuddled closer to Sawyer.

"You look great, sweetheart," Reese said as they walked to the car.

"Thanks, you do too!"

Reese grinned as they loaded the car up and then they were off. Blasting the heat, Claire held her hands to the vents, waiting for them to thaw as Reese navigated out of the airport. Pulling out her phone, she sent a quick text to Jude.

Claire: Landed and heading to the appointment you planned.

Jude: :) Hope you find the dress that will blow me away. I love you.

Her heart skipped a beat as she sent him back a smiley face along with that she loved him too and then leaned back in the car. She missed him like crazy but was glad to be home. Looking over at Reese, she smiled. Her aunt looked beautiful and almost like she was glowing. Her hair was up in a messy bun, and she wore light makeup with jeans and an Assassins tee. Even all comfy, she was beautiful. Reese had always thought she wouldn't be a good mom or wife, but she was both. The best, even.

"How's everyone?"

Reese grinned. "Good, big dinner tonight to welcome you home. Elli has been cooking all day."

"Great, I'm hungry," she said with a grin. "Can't wait to see everyone."

"They are excited to see you. Guess what?"

"What?"

"Harper is pregnant."

Sitting up erect, she shouted, "What?"

"Yup!"

"Oh my God! I thought she couldn't have any more kids."

"We all thought that, hell, she thought that, but she's ten weeks!"

Happiness and excitement poured out her pores as her grin grew. "That is so awesome."

"I know, we are all so excited. She's a blubbering mess, but she's not the only one."

"Really! Elli?"

Reese laughed. "Nope, the in vitro worked and Audrey's pregnant too."

"Awww. That's so awesome!

"Yeah, she isn't telling the world, but everyone who knows is pretty excited. Our little Assassins family is growing."

"This family has never been little," Claire said with a scoff, but she couldn't stop smiling. This was so awesome. All these women were basically aunts to her, and to know they were all getting their Happily Ever Afters was so fulfilling. She was next, and that made her giddy with excitement. "I'm so happy for everyone."

"Yeah," Reese agreed. "Also, Phillip and I have decided to start trying for another baby."

Gasping, Claire completely turned in her seat and shrieked. "What!"

Reese giggled. "Yup, I stopped taking birth control, so we will see."

"Eek! I am so excited!"

"We are too." Reese giggled as she pulled in the bridal shop parking lot. Getting out, Claire ran around and hugged Reese tightly which caused her to laugh. "I'm not pregnant yet."

"I know, but it's exciting. I love babies."

Reese's smiled dropped. "Doesn't mean you need one yet."

Claire laughed out loud, hard, and shook her head. "Believe me, not happening. We are gonna wait till my contract is done. I don't want to raise kids in Vegas."

"Thank sweet baby Jesus," Reese muttered as she got Sawyer out. Claire grinned as they made their way inside. They were greeted by a gorgeous blonde and then escorted back into a room. When they entered, Claire immediately saw the big bouquet of white roses and grinned. They were her favorite flower and Jude knew that.

"The groom has these waiting for you."

Reese awwed as Claire giggled. Going to the vase, she took in a big breath of them before grabbing the card and tearing it open.

Claire,

It was chance that I met you.
Fate that we fell in love.
And a blessing that you want to marry me.
I can't wait to be yours for the rest of my life.
Enjoy picking the dress that will be the start of our forever.
I love you.

Yours,
Jude.

"Oh my God," she gasped, covering her mouth. "He is so amazing."

Reese smiled as she took the card and read it, tears gathering in her eyes. "You need to frame this."

"I plan on it," Claire agreed, taking the card and tucking it back in the envelope. On cloud nine, she began searching for her dress, but she wasn't having any luck. She had tried on thirteen dresses and really didn't like any of them. She wanted something perfect. She wanted a forever kind of love dress.

Defeated, she let out a breath and met Reese's gaze.

"The dress might not be here."

"But yours was," Claire said and then she paused. She loved Reese's dress. Like, a lot. Turning slowly, she met Reese's gaze. "Wait. You're like my mom, right?"

Reese smiled. "Well, yeah."

"You know how brides wear their mom's dresses… So can I wear yours?"

Reese's eyes clouded with tears as she slowly nodded. "I would love that."

She wrapped her arms around Claire tightly, kissing her cheek. "I love you so much, Claire."

"So that's a yes?" she asked and Reese laughed.

"Yes, of course!"

Closing her eyes, Claire hugged Reese and knew this was the right choice. Phillip and Reese's love was something out of books, and her dress was gorgeous. It was a forever kind of love dress, and Claire couldn't think of anything else she'd rather wear than Reese's dress.

Her mom.

Being home was great. She spent time with her family, got to see some of her friends, and it was wonderful. But, she missed Jude. It was Christmas Eve night and Claire knew she should be happy, but she wasn't. She hated that she wasn't with him. Closing her eyes, she waited for him to answer as a tear rolled slowly down her cheek.

When he answered, she said, "I miss you."

His chuckle sent chills down her spine. "I miss you, baby, two more days."

"But you won't be here for presents or pie or anything. I'm going to be lonely without you."

"You will not. I bet Sawyer is driving you crazy."

"He is, but I miss you," she whined, wishing like hell that there was no distance between them. "I'm going to wake up and you won't be here on my favorite holiday."

"Wow, thanks for making me feel like an ass," he complained and she felt bad instantly.

"I'm sorry."

He laughed. "I know this sucks. It does, but I promise I'll make it up to you."

"No, I'm sorry, you're right, I'm being a brat. I just hate being apart. As soon as my contract is up, I'm done, and I swear you are going to have to peel me off you."

"I look forward to it. I love you, Claire. I do. So much."

"I love you more than that," she said with all the conviction in the world. Sometimes people picked at them saying they were so young and in love, but she loved it. She loved how intense they were about each other and couldn't wait until the moment they would be joined together as one. It would be the most amazing occasion of her life with everyone there to share in their love. They may be young, but they knew this was it. This was forever.

They talked for a little longer about his parents, and then she yawned, dead on her feet. She had gone shopping with Reese and Sawyer for last-minute gifts.

Laughing he said, "Okay, I'll call you tomorrow before the game."

She smiled as she pushed back her tears. "I'll be watching."

"Good. Enjoy your gifts tomorrow."

"I wish you were one of them. That would be so hot, you under the tree with a bow."

He chuckled. "I was thinking the same thing, but you with bows on your naughty bits."

She giggled as heat engulfed her. "Don't turn me on if you can't get me off."

He scoffed. "Oh, baby, I can get you off with just my words, but I don't want you coming, screaming in your uncle's house. He already wants to kill me ninety-nine percent of the time."

She giggled. "But hey, that one percent, he likes you."

"I doubt that, but he'll like me soon enough."

"Sure," she agreed and he laughed.

"Okay, I love you. Call you tomorrow."

"Love you too."

When she hung up, the sadness was there, but this was the life she'd chosen. Hockey players came and went on the holidays, so she'd better get used to it. Especially since she was about to marry one.

"Claire! Claire! Claire!"

Claire slowly opened one eye to see Sawyer on her chest, smacking her with his palms.

Stretching, since this wasn't the first time her little guy had done this, she said, "What, honey?"

"Santa came!"

She smiled as she cuddled into him. She needed the comfort because when she was out of the bed, it would mean that she was spending Christmas without

Jude. She really didn't want to accept that, but Sawyer was wiggling and then was dragging her out of the bed.

"Come on, Claire-bear! Santa came!"

"I know, buddy, but I don't want to," she complained, kissing his hands.

"But you have to!" he protested, pulling her.

Knowing that he was going away and that Phillip and Reese were probably waiting on her, she got out of bed with a huff. "You owe me hot chocolate, kid."

"With peppers!"

She smiled. "Yes, with peppermint."

She took his hand and they made their way through to the kitchen where Reese was standing.

"Merry Christmas, honey."

Claire shrugged. "Be way merrier if Jude were here."

Reese smiled as she shrugged. "Don't be a Grinch."

Claire giggled as Sawyer said, "Yeah, don't be a Grinch!"

"Claire being a Grinch?" Phillip asked, coming into the kitchen with a coffee cup in hand. "Maybe we should send her to the North Pole?"

Sawyer agreed. "Yeah, Santa needs to put the Christmas in her!"

"Sorry, I'm a little down. I'll perk up, give me hot chocolate," she said, picking up her little guy just as Reese handed her a cup. Music was playing, which wasn't odd, but the song made her a little sad. "I'll Be Home for Christmas" was the song, and usually she liked it, but today she could do without hearing it.

"You have to be happy. Santa brought you something," Sawyer said.

She scoffed. "Santa always skips me."

"Nooooooo, not this time, come on!" He wiggled and she put him down. He pulled her into the living room, and when her eyes caught sight of the present, she squealed. Sitting by the tree with a huge red bow on his head was Jude.

"Jude!"

His face broke out in a grin as he stood, catching her as she jumped into his arms. Covering his mouth with hers, she kissed him deeply as her heart came out of her chest. Holding her close, he smiled against her lips as he spun her around. Pulling back, he grinned down at her, the bow falling into his sweet, gorgeous eyes. Elated, she asked, "What are you doing here?"

"They canceled the game because no one can fly into New York, it's snowing so bad. So instead of going back to California with the guys, I came home. You wanted me under your tree, so that's where I wanted to be."

Kissing him again, she wrapped her arms around his neck and almost started to cry. Kissing her jaw, he then kissed her nose and smiled, his heart beating against hers. She couldn't get over how gorgeous he was, and he was all hers. She had missed him so much and he was there. In the flesh, on Christmas with her. There could be a million gifts under the tree, but the most important gift was looking deep into her eyes with his arms holding her tight to him.

"Merry Christmas, Claire."

She grinned as she looked into the eyes of her forever. "Merry Christmas, indeed."

The Adler residence not only looked like Santa crapped all over it with Christmas decorations but it also looked like a tornado had gone through it. Wrapping paper and toys covered every square inch of their living room, but Shea Adler didn't care.

His family was happy.

Like they had done for the last seven years, they woke up at the butt-crack of dawn and surrounded the tree, passing out gifts. With each year, it became more hectic though. When it had been just him and his gorgeous wife, Elli, it was easy but consisted of a lot of sex under the tree. Then Shelli came, again easy. Then Posey, still easy, but when the twins came, things started to get a little rowdy. By the time Quinn came, it was a mess. Lots of tearing of wrapping paper and lots of screaming, but he didn't care. The kids were always happy.

And he actually liked the chaos.

"Mommy, I love it! Thank you! Daddy, you're the greatest!" Shelli exclaimed as she held up her new iPad.

"But I want an iPad, Daddy!" Posey complained.

"Open the box, honey," Shea said softly. She did then gave him a sheepish grin.

"Thank you, Daddy," she giggled, holding up her iPad.

"You're welcome, honey," he said as Elli leaned against him.

She looked gorgeous with her hair a mess and in his big Assassins tee with long pants. Her feet were covered by the new reindeer socks Quinn had gotten her. She had on earmuffs the girls had given her and also gloves the twins had picked out.

"Warm and toasty?" he asked and she grinned.

"Oh yes, my kiddos give the best gifts, don't you think?"

He chuckled as she looked him over. He was wearing a big, bright purple scarf that the girls had selected, along with knee-high hockey socks that the twins had gotten him, and reindeer slippers. He looked like a total loser, but he wore his gifts with pride. "I say I think you are right."

She smiled before leaning up to press her lips to his. Wrapping her arms around his neck, she leaned her forehead against his jaw as they watched the kids tear open presents and cheer when they got something they wanted. He always loved when they got clothes though. Their faces were priceless. Especially Owen's. He didn't hold anything back and made sure they all knew that a gift wasn't what he wanted. Shelli was kind and always thanked them for things even if she didn't want it. Which didn't happen a lot.

Just to mess with her though, he got her a Ninja Turtle, and when she opened it, she asked if it was for one of the boys. He told her no, it was for her, and her face was something for the books. He'd never laughed so hard in his life before telling her it was his, when really, he was going to give it to one of the rookies. The other kids were just happy to get to open presents, and he enjoyed that they were so ecstatic. They still had Christmas with his family later that night, and they were even going to Elli's dad's house the following day, which would be awkward because her mom and sister would be there. Since they were still trying to suck up to Elli, he was sure that they would get something overly extravagant for the kids, and he hated that. They didn't have to buy the kids' love or Elli's, they just had to be good to them.

That was obviously hard for Victoria and Olivia Fisher.

Kissing his beautiful wife's forehead, he said, "Wanna open my gift?"

"You got me something?" she asked sweetly and he smiled.

"You know I did. You probably already know what it is," he said, getting up and going to the tree to retrieve the gift.

"I really don't," she reassured him as he handed her the large box. "Shelli, baby, hand me Daddy's gift."

"Got me something?" he teased and she shot him a grin.

"You know I did. I love Christmas."

That she did. It was her favorite holiday, and that was one of the main reason he wished they weren't going to Michael Fisher's house. He didn't want her sister and mother to ruin Elli's favorite holiday.

When the kids stopped opening their gifts and gathered around them, Shea nodded toward Elli for her to go.

"No, you go first," she said, basically jumping in her seat. "I'm so excited for you to see what it is."

To please her, he nodded and opened the box. It was a watch box, and when he opened it to the expensive-looking watch, he smiled. "Thank you. I needed a new watch."

"That's not even the best part, look at the base."

His brows pulled together as he focused on the watch to see that it not only had the time but a picture of Elli and the kids. "And the inscription," she added.

He smiled as he read the inside of the watch: *To the best daddy in the world. We love you. So much.*

His grin grew as he put the watch on, looking over at Elli. "I love it. Thank you."

He then leaned over, kissing her lips as the kids giggled and some said ew. Parting, she grinned as she bounced in her seat.

"Your turn."

"What is it?" she asked as she pulled the wrapping off.

"A horse," Shea deadpanned and she giggled. "Open it and see."

Her grin was unstoppable as she torn open the box. When she looked inside, he smiled when a perplexed look came over her face. Pulling out a smaller box, she glanced at him and he chuckled.

"You thought it was that mixer, huh?"

"Maybe," she said slowly as she started to unwrap the smaller box.

"It's under the tree," he answered and her face lit up.

"Then what is this?"

"Open it and see."

The kids were basically bouncing off the walls in anticipation. Everyone knew what he had gotten her, and it had taken almost a year to plan. He was excited to see what she thought, though. Opening the box, her brows came together as she took in what she was looking at.

"Are these plane tickets?"

He nodded as she pulled them out.

"To Fiji?" she asked but then separated the tickets. "There are only two here."

"Because only you and I are going. For a week."

"What? I can't leave the kids or even the team! You're crazy."

"Mom and Dad are going to come stay with the kids, and I already cleared it at work. We are leaving after New Year's."

"What!" she gasped, looking at him in disbelief. "Really?"

His hand came down on her thigh and he smiled. "We haven't had a vacation since Shelli was born. I think it's time we had some us time, don't you think?"

When she looked up at him, tears gathering in her eyes, he knew he had done good. Great, even. "Yeah. I think so," she agreed, wiping her eyes. "A whole week? Just us? No yelling, boogers, or hockey?"

He laughed. "Just us and the beach. We are staying in a hut with no one around but a guy to give us food and drinks."

"Sounds like paradise."

"It will be."

"Oh my God, I can't wait! Thank you!" she cried, wrapping her arms around his neck and kissing him hard on the lips. When she parted, she was frowning though. "I only got you a watch."

He scoffed. "Baby, you've given me the world and then some. Now it's my turn to give you everything you can dream of."

"You do that every day, Shea, just by loving me," she said, tears rolling down her beautiful face. Her eyes still hit him straight in the gut, and her lips could knock him to his knees. She was everything and more. He would give her anything she asked without even really thinking.

"I love you," she whispered, her lips ever so close to his. "More than words could express."

"I love you."

"Group hug!" Shelli exclaimed, and soon all five of their children jumped in where they could fit in. With Shelli in his lap, Quinn on his back, and Evan around his waist, he looked into the eyes of his forever and smiled. Elli was holding Posey and Owen close but still holding him too, a beautiful, happy grin on her face.

"Daddy, I love you," Shelli said, kissing his cheek. "I love you too, Momma."

"Yeah, I love you," Quinn said.

"Me too, I love y'all," Owen said.

"I love you so much. Thank you for my presents," Posey said softly.

"I love you more than they do," Evan informed them, ever serious but the instigator of the family. Soon everyone was protesting on who loved whom more.

Finally, Elli said, "Guys, stop. I love you all. The exact same. You are all the world to me."

They all grinned and seemed content with that. Looking over at Elli, Shea smiled, holding her jaw. "You happy, baby?"

She nodded, kissing his nose. "So much so, it hurts, Shea. You've given me everything I could have ever asked for."

His heart pounded in his chest as he got lost in her eyes. How did he get this lucky? To find his soul mate and not only marry her but make beautiful children with her. Kissing her nose, he said, "And to think, I still have the rest of our lives to give you even more."

Her grin grew as her eyes clouded with tears and she said, "Merry Christmas, my love."

"Merry Christmas."

Of course, Elli forgot a present. It was her luck. It wasn't bad enough she had to go deal with her mother and sister, but she forgot to get something for Karson and Lacey King. This was so unlike her, but she blamed it totally on everyone else.

In the weeks leading up to Christmas, she had been so busy. Fallon had had her baby, so of course, she had to go over and love on her little Emery. After making sure her house was clean, Fallon was comfy, and food was cooked, Elli spent some time at work. The boys had hockey, Shelli had dance, and Posey had gymnastics. Quinn, poor guy, had to go everywhere with her and bitched about it relentlessly.

Then she found out Audrey was pregnant after years of trying. Apparently, it was the year of Christmas miracles because so was Harper, which was just mind-blowing. Being the friend she was, she went over and loved on them, made sure they had everything they needed and picked dates for baby showers. Since, of course, she would be planning them. Then Claire came home from Vegas, so she cooked a huge dinner and invited everyone over to celebrate not only her homecoming but the fact that she had picked a date for her wedding, and it was right around the corner! After making sure Claire knew that her aunt Elli would do everything and anything to help with the wedding, she worked, was the kids' driver, and then did loads and loads of homework. Between all that, she had to reassure Piper that she could be a book cover designer and no one would think she was a flake, she had to trade away two players, and then she had to make sure her husband was sexually satisfied.

To say the Elli Adler was a busy woman was a damn understatement.

So while it wasn't a surprise that she forgot to buy a gift for their friends, she was still disappointed in herself. But then she thought about sitting on the beach for a whole week. No kids, no hockey crap, no friends to take care of, and really, she wouldn't even have to think. All she had to do was drink fruity drinks, eat food, and have sex with her husband over and over again. It sounded like the most amazing vacation in the world, and she was counting down the days. All she had to do was get through this dinner with her family, the Assassins' New Year's Eve party, and then she would be on a plane to Fiji with her hot as sin husband.

Since her sexy husband was at practice, she had all the kids in tow as they rushed through Bass Pro Shop. Apparently Lacey had never gone hunting before and Karson had been trying to talk her into going. Elli's uncle had a cabin in the woods out in Clarksville, so she decided to buy them a gift card to the pro shop so they could come and stock up for their little adventure that the Adler family was going to give them.

She held Shelli's and Quinn's hands, and they held on to the other kids as they navigated through the shop. She also needed to get a gun cleaning kit for her daddy, and she needed to get home to wrap everything, but this place was packed with people trying to get day after Christmas sales. This was a horrible idea.

"Momma! The fish tanks!" Quinn exclaimed.

"Yeah, Momma, can we stop! Please," Owen begged.

"Please!" the other three chimed.

"Yes, of course. Come on, five minutes. We gotta go, my loves."

"Okay!" they all chorused before running off to look at the fish tank. Crossing her arms across the stomach, she watched as the kids oohed and aahed over the fish. She loved watching them when they were interested in something. Each one was so different, it was insane. Even Evan and Owen were completely different. Shelli was her overachiever, pleaser, while Posey did what she wanted and didn't care what anyone said. Owen was her quiet one, while Evan was her loud, obnoxious one, and Quinn was just downright insane. That's the only way she could describe him.

Counting each one, she started to panic when she didn't see Quinn.

"Shelli! Where is Quinn?"

"Right here, looking at the bear, Momma," she said, pointing to her baby brother, and when Elli saw him, her heart calmed. The bear was blocking her view of him. Sheesh, she almost had a mini heart attack. Letting out a breath, she smiled, thanking the good Lord above, but then in true Quinn fashion, he yelled to her.

"Momma!"

She looked back at him to scold him for yelling, but she was speechless by what she saw. Quinn's pants were around his ankles, his hand holding his penis, and his other holding the bear's big damn penis.

"Momma! Look, it's got a dick like me!"

"Quinn!" Shelli yelled, her hand covering her mouth as the boys lost their shit laughing.

"Oh. My. Goodness! Momma! Quinn is playing with his no-no!" Posey yelled and Elli couldn't move. This was not happening. She was frozen in place as everyone stopped to look and laugh.

"Hell's Bells, Quinn! Pull your pants up!"

"I swear, I have never been so embarrassed in my life! Holding his penis, screaming he and the bear both have a dick in the middle of the pro shop. A dick, Shea! That is your fault, I swear to goodness. I am so mad and freaking embarrassed."

Looking across the island at her husband who was obviously holding in his laughter, Elli just got madder. "Speak, Shea Ryan Adler!"

"Yeah, I don't have anything."

"Nothing?"

He held up his hands. "I won't use the word dick in this house ever again, and if anyone says it around our kids, I'll punch them in the di—penis."

Glaring, she whipped around to go to the fridge. "I swear to goodness. You have no clue what that was like. It was so horrible."

When his arms came around her waist, she closed her eyes as she leaned back into him. Kissing up her neck, he nibbled at her earlobe before whispering, "I'm sorry you were embarrassed by our insane three-year-old."

She knew how silly it was to be embarrassed, but everyone saw her little boy's penis, along with the fact that he was holding on to a bear's. The horror. Shaking her head, she let out a breath. "I was just so surprised by it all."

"It happens. They are crazy. All of them."

She giggled. "But they are all ours."

"And I wouldn't trade them in for anything. Dicks and all."

Closing her eyes, she laughed for the first time as Shea chuckled in her ear. Turning in his arms, she kissed his lips, melting against him. He could still take every bit of stress out of her body with one kiss. That was probably why she hadn't lost her damn mind yet. Because Shea loved her. More than she would ever deserve.

"We have to go to my dad's."

"Yay," he said, but she didn't miss that he wasn't excited.

"Yeah. My sentiments exactly. Let's go."

When they arrived at her family home, her stomach sank. She'd much rather go back to the pro shop and let Quinn helicopter his penis around the damn store than deal with her mother and sister. She had dressed to the nines and even had the kids dress supernice just so her family wouldn't have anything to say. Well, more her mother than anything.

When her father took her mother back six months ago, Elli thought it was a bad idea, but apparently, she had turned over a new leaf. She acted nice as all get out and loved on her kids like she cared, but she could see in Olivia's eyes that she didn't care one bit. She just missed the money her daddy had. She hated thinking that of her mother, but it was the truth. The woman didn't care one bit about Elli or her children; it was about the security her father offered her.

Victoria, well, Elli didn't talk to her. Victoria didn't try, and Elli wasn't sure if she was good to the kids because she wanted to be or because she was trying to get money out of their father. Elli just wasn't sure. Shea didn't like any of them, but like the good sport he was, he sat through dinner and said nice things when he was asked something. Elli, on the other hand, only talked when she was talked to. Which wasn't much.

"Elli, darling, you're looking thin," Olivia then said, and everyone stopped eating to look down at her.

"Momma is beautiful," Evan informed her, turkey hanging from his mouth.

"Yeah, like all the time," Shelli added.

"She's the best too," Posey said with a nod.

"I agree, kiddos. I think your momma is the prettiest girl ever," her father said with a wink. She smiled but didn't miss the looks Olivia and Victoria gave him. It was easy to say you could cut the tension with a knife.

"Y'all sure do love your momma," Olivia said with a big ol' fake grin on her face.

"Ugh, yeah, she's our momma," Evan said with a look on his face that said he thought she was an idiot. "Duh."

"Evan Marcus, that's rude," Shea reprimanded and Evan nodded.

"Yes, sir. Sorry, Grandma."

"Oh, you're fine!" she said, way too quickly, in Elli's opinion.

Elli smiled as she laced her fingers with Evan's. "Well, I sure do love y'all, and thank you, Mother."

That ended the conversation, and shortly after dinner, they were gathered around the big Christmas tree, opening gifts. Sitting in Shea's lap, Elli moved her fingers along his jaw as she watched her little bits open the presents her family had gotten them. Of course, they spoiled them and Elli hated it. She wished they were more involved than just buying them things. Minus her father, of course. Elli would never think that of her father.

"I love you," Shea whispered in her ear, and she grinned as she leaned her head against his.

"I love you."

"Good, can you go get me another beer, please?"

She giggled as she shook her head. "You're ridiculous."

"I need beer. I have to be at least almost drunk to deal with your mother," he said softly with all the seriousness in the world.

"Touché," she said with a nod before getting up to head to the kitchen. "Daddy, do you need another beer?"

"Sure, my sweetheart, thank you," he said with a wink. She kissed his cheek before heading through her childhood home. Soon she noticed that nothing had changed. Her dad had let it go some since he had been drowning himself with work, but she was sure it would not stay that way with Olivia back home. She would have this place back to pristine condition in no time. Probably the only good thing about her mother returning.

Taking frozen mugs out of the freezer, she poured two beers and threw the cans away. As she turned to leave, she paused when she almost came crashing into Victoria. Her sister was all legs and still as gorgeous as ever. Long, dark auburn hair curled down her shoulders, her green eyes were wicked, and her lips devastating to any man who came in contact.

Meeting her gaze, Elli looked away quickly and said, "Sorry."

"It's fine," Victoria said, but she didn't move. "Can I talk to you for a moment?"

Elli's brows came up as she set the mugs on the counter. "Um, yeah, I guess."

Victoria cleared her throat and looked down at her hands. "We haven't spoken much since everything went down."

"No, we haven't."

"Yeah, well, I…well, you see, I—" she stopped and took in a deep breath before meeting Elli's questioning gaze. "I want to change that. I don't want to fight. I don't want you to be mad at me. I want to be able to see my nieces and nephews. I want a relationship with you."

Elli's brows came in. Huh? "Why?"

Victoria smiled, but Elli could tell she was uncomfortable. Clearing her throat, she said, "Because I've learned being a bitch drives everyone away. I'm trying to change and fix the wrong I've done. I'm sorry for everything I've ever done to you. The name-calling, the putting you down, the trying to ruin you and Shea. I was wrong, and I am very sorry for that."

Elli could only blink as her older sister, who she'd always thought was Satan, slowly started to cry.

"I adore your children. They are beautiful souls, and I really would like the chance to spend more time with them and you. I want us to be sisters, not strangers."

Looking away, Elli took in a sharp breath. This was completely crazy. They hadn't spoken more than two sentences to each other in almost eight years. "I'm sorry, but this has kind of left me speechless."

"I know," Victoria agreed. "I don't deserve your trust, or even for you to accept my apology, but I promise, I am being true and speaking from the heart. I'm not under Mom's control anymore. I'm my own woman. I don't need anyone anymore, but I want to have you and the kids in my life."

Her eyes were sincere, and this was the first time Elli had ever seen her sister look at her like that. Elli didn't know if she could trust her, but she kinda wanted to. She had always wanted a real, loving relationship with Victoria. She'd envied her when she was growing up and wished that she would have given her the time of day. Kind of like how Harper was with her baby sisters. She wanted that, and maybe this was her chance.

Or maybe it would all blow up in her face. She wasn't sure, but slowly she nodded, a grin pulling at her lips as she said, "I would like that. Maybe we can get together for coffee when I get back from Fiji."

Victoria's lip quivered as she nodded, her eyes not leaving Elli's. "I would really love that."

"Why are you looking at me like that?" Elli said with a laugh later that night as she lay beside her husband in bed.

"Because why would you agree to go to have coffee with the person who tried to break us up?"

"Because she is my sister."

"So what, next is your mom?"

Elli shook her head. "My mom hasn't apologized, Victoria did, and she wants to know me and have a relationship with me. It can't hurt to give it a shot."

He looked skeptical as he shrugged. "Just be careful."

"I will, and plus Christmas is a time for forgiving and loving thy neighbor."

"I doubt that neighbor schemed against you and kissed your boyfriend to make you break up with him."

Elli smiled as she hooked a leg over his hip. "Probably not, but we overcame it."

"After three months of hell. Took me busting some glass and paying a fine to get you to listen to me," he added.

"But look at us now!"

He chuckled as he gathered her in his arms. "Yeah, look at us. Happy, kids, the whole nine yards huh?"

She nodded, her fingers tangling in the hairs at the nape of his neck. "It's a pretty great life."

"I couldn't agree more, and to think, I get a whole week to make love to you every second of the day."

"Mmmm," she purred against his lips. "The great thing is I can't get pregnant either."

That had them both laughing, shaking the bed as their laughter filled the room. Gathering her in his arms, he kissed her nose and then one side of her mouth and the other before her lips. As her heart pounded against her ribs, she couldn't think of another place she'd rather be than in Shea Adler's arms. She wasn't sure of the future, but as long as it was with Shea and her kiddos, she'd be just fine.

Christmas had been an eventful one, but she wouldn't have had it any other way. It was her life—eventful and crazy with her clan of kids and mind-blowing husband. She wasn't sure how she got this fortunate, but she thanked the good Lord above as her husband slowly peeled her clothes away before making sweet love to her. It was a blessing to not only wake up being the wife of her gorgeous husband but the mother of five of the best kids on this planet. And as her husband slowly moved inside of her, his eyes trained on hers, Elli Adler knew that life couldn't get any better.

She had it all.

Karson & LACEY

"Kacey, you've been on that phone all damn afternoon. Put it the hell down!"

Lacey King giggled as her mother-in-law, Regina, tried to knock her daughter's phone out of her hand.

"Ma! Stop!" Kacey yelled back. "This is important!"

"What could be so damn important that you'd rather be on that phone than talk to us?"

"Duh, Ma, a dude," she informed her, looking at her mother with a deadpan expression.

Lacey giggled as she shook her head. Having her in-laws home was a blessing in disguise. She loved them, but man, they were loud.

"A dude?" Regina asked, a little taken aback. "Who?"

Kacey's grin grew and Lacey smiled. Her sister-in-law was a beautiful woman. Strong as an ox and built like one too. Her eyes were like razors, sharp and beautiful, while her hair was finally touching her shoulders. Since Karson, her brother and Lacey's husband, constantly said she was a lesbian, Lacey had noticed that Kacey had started to grow her hair out. If she was a showstopper with short hair, Lord help the male gender when she grew it out.

"No one," she said, waving her off before tucking her phone in her pocket. "I'm done. What's up?"

"Well, I'm trying to talk Lacey into having a baby. Help me," Regina said and Lacey just giggled.

"Ma, please, they'll do it when they want to," Kacey said with a shake of her head. "But please, Lacey, pop one out so she'll shut up."

Lacey grinned as she shrugged. "I can say we aren't preventing it, but we aren't trying. We are giving it to the Lord."

"I love her," Regina said with a dreamy look on her face. "She's a great woman: smart and beautiful and God-fearing. We picked a good one for our Karson."

Lacey laughed as she shook her head. "I'm pretty sure he picked me."

"Yes, but we decided to keep you," Regina said with a wink before kissing Lacey's cheek. "Best decision ever. Now we just need Kacey to find a good man."

Kacey scoffed at that. "Please. There are no good men in the world. Daddy and Karson have set the bar too high."

"Agreed," Lacey said, sending Kacey a grin. "But yours is out there."

"Eh, I'm good with my life."

"That's all that matters," Lacey said before Regina could object to that.

"I'm gonna take these to the men," Regina said, taking the meals that Lacey had just plated and leaving for the living room.

Smiling contentedly, Lacey took a sip of her tea as she looked around the kitchen. She loved this kitchen. She loved her house. She loved Nashville. But most of all, she loved Karson so much. The last month had been perfect. They couldn't be more in love, and everything was moving great for them. They were still looking for a location to expand Lacey's Lace, but she knew in her heart that the right place was there, and when she found it, it was on.

She couldn't wait to open the new store. She decided that Rachel would be the manager of the one in Chicago, and she would take over running the one in Nashville. Thinking of Rachel, she smiled. She and Grady had left two days ago after spending Christmas with Lacey and the Kings. Lacey was surprised when her brother said that he wanted to spend Christmas in Nashville because that meant they wouldn't be spending it with their dad since Lacey still wasn't talking to him.

It had been tough, but she stood by what she said. She wouldn't let him ruin her. Since she wasn't talking to him, she guessed he realized that he would have to really prove that he wasn't going to try to break her and Karson up because he had been on his best behavior. Every day she got an email from him asking how she was. He sent flowers and elaborate gifts for Christmas. He even sent Karson a new hockey stick. Karson joked that it had anthrax on it, but she did think it was a start. Still though, she didn't call him. She sent him a very short email saying thank you, but that she wasn't ready to talk to him.

And she wasn't. She wasn't sure when she would be either. He'd broken her heart, but thankfully, Karson put it back together. She refused to be unhappy, so she cut out the bad. Fortunately, things between her and Rachel were good after a very long talk. She knew that her dad had been manipulating Rachel; Lacey just wished Rachel wouldn't have given in to him. Rachel's need for a father figure was insane, but Lacey was glad she opened her eyes and saw that Lacey's father was not the father figure she needed. He wasn't a father figure at all. He was a controlling bastard, and Lacey wouldn't have any part of it.

While losing her father in her life sucked, she was relieved that she and Grady had gotten closer. He still talked to their father, but it was for the boys more than anything. She didn't understand how he could be so good to his grandsons but not to his children. It was mind-blowing, but Lacey had made peace with it. She had Karson and his parents if she needed parental figures. Regina and Karl King loved her like she was theirs, and that was more than she could ever wish for.

Plus, she had a new sister. She and Kacey had gotten very close over the last couple weeks, and she knew exactly who Kacey had been speaking to the whole time she had been in Karson and Lacey's home.

"I thought you said you were going to break it off?"

Kacey grinned as she met Lacey's gaze. "I would, but ugh, the sex is so good."

Lacey giggled before setting her with a look. "He doesn't want a relationship."

"I know," she said, letting her shoulders fall. "I need to break it off."

"Yeah, you do. Jordie Thomas is not a take-home-to-Momma kind of man."

"No, he isn't," she agreed. "But he is a fuck-you-stupid kind of man."

Lacey laughed out loud as images of JT having sex with some girl in the living room came to mind. "Unfortunately, I know exactly what you mean."

Kacey knew all about the first time Lacey met JT and proceeded to laugh her butt off while Lacey shuddered. Looking over at her, Lacey said, "You know Karson will flip if he finds out."

"Yeah, but I'm gonna stop. I have to."

Lacey eyed her as she picked at the sandwich that was in front of her. Kacey's eyes were sad and she looked defeated, and Lacey wasn't sure why. That was until it dawned on her. "You've fallen for him."

Kacey didn't even look at her as she slowly nodded. "Yup, like a dumbass."

"Oh, Kacey," she said, covering her sister-in-law's hand with hers. "Let it go before it gets unbearable."

"I'm going to."

Before Lacey could say more, her phone rang and she saw that it was her brother. "Oh, excuse me, it's Grady."

"Cool, I'll go in the living room."

Answering it, she said, "Hold on, Grady." She then looked at Kacey. "You don't have to."

"It's cool. I'm gonna go be masochistic and keep texting the guy who will never love me back."

Lacey's heart sank as she watched Kacey walk away. Letting out a breath, she said into the phone, "Hey, sorry, hey!"

Grady chuckled. "Hey, so I'm calling because I was told to ask you something, and you're probably not going to like what I have to ask."

"Ew, what?" she asked, knowing darn well that her dad had probably told Grady to call her.

"Well, Dad is wondering if you and Karson are going to come to his and Sabrina's wedding in March."

"It's in March," she deadpanned. "Why do I have to answer now?"

"I don't know, and honestly, I don't even want to go. I don't like Sabrina."

"Who does?"

He laughed. "Exactly, but I figured he is our dad, so we should support him."

"He doesn't support me though."

Grady didn't say anything for a second and then said, "You're right, and I completely understand if you don't want to go. Do you want me to just say no now and save you the deciding?"

She chewed on her lip for a moment as she leaned against the counter. Did she go or not?

When a pair of arms wrapped around her stomach, she melted against her husband and looked at him with a small smile on her lips. Looking at her, his brows drew in and he asked, "What's wrong?"

"Grady wants to know if we are going to my dad's wedding."

Karson stiffened against her, and she knew the answer without his even answering her.

"No, we aren't going," she answered, moving her hand up to hold Karson's face.

"Completely understandable. Don't even know why I called, really. I knew the answer before I picked up the phone."

She smiled. "No biggie, always good to hear from you."

"Yeah, by the way, again, thanks for having us. It was a wonderful time."

"It was. You guys are always welcome."

"Thanks. Okay, well, Zander is pulling me to the garage, so I'll call you later. Love you."

"Love you," she answered back before hanging up the phone. Turning in Karson's arms, she kissed his jaw. "I love you, husband."

He smiled as his hand traveled down her body to her ass. "I love you, wife. You okay?"

She nodded. "Of course. I didn't want to go anyway. I don't want to watch my dad marry someone else."

"And because he is an asshole," Karson added and Lacey smiled.

"That too," she agreed, holding him closer to her. "Anyone who tries to take you away from me isn't worth my time."

"I couldn't agree more," he whispered, kissing the top of her head. He held her for a long time, and as she closed her eyes, she didn't want to be anywhere but in her husband's strong arms. Kissing his chest, she snuggled closer and just felt complete. So much had changed since she'd met him. Her life had been completely turned upside down. It used to scare her, but now, she knew there was no other way. She was meant to love Karson Jett King, and everything else just fell into place.

"My mom is driving me crazy. I wish you wouldn't have told her that we aren't trying but we aren't preventing. She seriously just told me to make sure to hold your legs up after sex. It was awkward."

Lacey giggled against his chest as she shook her head. "Your mother is a hoot."

"No, she's batshit crazy."

Laughing harder now, she looked at him and couldn't fathom how much she loved him. It was as natural as breathing, and he was everything she could ever wish for. Their first Christmas had been magnificent. They had beautiful, hot sex and then rushed downstairs where Regina was cooking a hefty breakfast. After eating with their families, they opened presents and enjoyed being together. She loved watching her nephews open presents and could honestly see a child of their own ripping paper away to find the gift that Mommy and Daddy had gotten them.

It was insane that she had been so against the idea of having her own baby before. It was the fear, but now, she wouldn't say she wasn't scared still, but she was open to the idea. Karson was right when he said they would raise a fighter because she was one. She had started counseling, and it was helping so much. Especially since Karson sat right next to her and held her hand as she relived all the horror the cancer brought on. They talked out everything and she felt much better. She even joined an After Breast Cancer program at the YMCA. She wished she had done it years ago, but she felt like a whole different person now that she had been getting help.

She not only felt like a better woman but also a better wife, and maybe one day, a great mom. Like her mom had been. Looking deep into Karson's eyes, she knew that as long as she was with him, she would be the best.

Because he brought out the greatness in her.

As she did for him.

Karson loved his wife.

He was convinced he was the luckiest man on earth to be able to watch her make her way down the stairs of their home looking like a billion bucks. In a gold sequined dress that was long-sleeved and hugged every single inch of her sexy body, her legs went on for days in black tights with high black heels. Her hair was up in a twist and her makeup was dramatic and smoky, bringing out the flecks of gold in her green eyes. She was stunning.

And all fucking his.

"Damn, woman! I'm supposed to take you out when you are that damn hot?"

A sneaky grin came over her face as she took his hand. "Yes. I spent two hours getting this hot. You are taking me out."

His heart pounding in his chest as he brought her in close, his mouth dusted against her glossed-up lips. "Or, I can take you upstairs and ring in the new year by banging into you."

She gasped against his lips as his hands cupped her sweet ass. "While I would love that—because you know they say what you are doing and who you are with on New Year's is how you'll spend that year, I have to say, I want to go out and enjoy the night that Fallon has worked so hard on," she said and he groaned in protest. "Plus, we find out if Kacey makes the team tonight, and if we are banging all night, we won't answer the phone."

He smiled as he nodded. "Smart woman I am married to."

"Damn right," she said, kissing his lips. "Now off we go. I want to shake my booty!"

She pulled from his grip, but he snatched her back in, pressing his growing erection against the swell of her ass and nipping at her earlobe. "No shaking. I can't handle that."

Her laughter was airy. "Why not? Won't it turn you on?"

"More than you'll ever know, and then I'll be hard all night wanting to be inside that sweet ass."

"Mmm," she moaned as his fingers danced on the outside of her thighs. Slowly she moved her ass against him but then broke away, a teasing grin on her face. "Guess you'll have to want me all night."

He scoffed "Baby, I want you every fucking second of the day. Come here, let me get a piece real quick."

"No way. We are leaving, come on," she said, walking away quickly and then out the door without waiting for him.

Man. She drove him insane.

And he loved every second of it.

The Assassins' New Year's party was the biggest event of the year.

Fallon Brooks put on one hell of a party, and Karson was always impressed by her skills. The party was covered in purple and black, the Assassins' colors. The Christmas tree that was so tall it reached the roof of the arena was covered in Assassins memorabilia. Each guy's jersey adorned the tree and then pictures of the guys with their families brought something special to it. Before, it used to be a picture of just Karson with his family, but this year, it was a picture of him and Lacey in front of their tree, completely and utterly in love.

He loved these parties; he got to drink it up and shoot the shit with his brothers. Most of the guys were married to unbelievable women, and the guys who weren't brought their little hot dates, trying to outdo each other in a friendly game. It blew his mind how, in such a short time, everything had changed for him. He used to be that guy, bringing the hottest chick he could in the hopes of outdoing all his other single teammates.

Now though, he was outdoing all the married guys because his wife was smoking.

Wrapping his arm around Lacey's middle, he smiled as she gushed to Audrey and Tate Odder.

"I am so excited for you!"

Audrey's eyes were misty as she smiled in thanks. "It's insane and so amazing, but I am really freaking pregnant and so damn sick!"

"Do you know if it is just one or two or four?" Lacey asked, her eyes bright.

Audrey nodded. "The ultrasound showed only one. It's our little fighter."

"That's so beautiful! Karson, isn't that awesome?" she asked him and he nodded.

"So awesome, I'm not sure who I am more surprised by, you or Harper."

Audrey nodded, throwing her hands up. "I know, right? I can't believe it!"

"Everyone is pregnant. Do you remember Jordan Ryan?" Tate asked, and Karson thought for a second.

"He was the goalie before you took over, right? Over on Carolina now."

"Yeah, his wife is pregnant with their second daughter. She's due in a couple weeks."

He didn't know Jordan well, but he nodded his head as Audrey cried out, "So many babies are coming!"

"We are always having babies on this team though," Karson laughed.

"Y'all are next!" she said with a promising grin, and Karson's arm tightened around Lacey.

"If it happens, it does, if it doesn't, then I'll try harder," he said and everyone laughed while Lacey beamed up at him. They talked for a little bit longer and then moved on to where Shea and Elli were.

"Baby, do you need a drink? You haven't touched anything yet," he asked before reaching his captain and his boss.

"I'm gonna let you drink tonight," she said, waving him off. "My belly is a little upset all of a sudden."

"You hungry?" he asked. "I know how you get when you don't eat. I duck and hide."

She rolled her eyes. "Shut up, and maybe I'll go make a plate. Talk with Elli and Shea for a second. I'll be back," she said before pressing her lips to his and then heading for the buffet.

"Hey, get me a turkey leg!" he called after her, and she nodded as Elli grinned at him.

"Having fun, Karson?" she asked and he smiled as he kissed her cheek. She looked gorgeous in a floor-length green dress that made her eyes shine. He'd always had a soft spot for Elli. Or maybe he was deathly scared of Shea and wanted to stay in their good graces. He wasn't sure, but they had been spending a lot of time with the Adlers. Lacey loved Elli and their kids, so did he, so it wasn't a hardship to hang out. Especially with the way Elli cooked. She could fry the hell out of some chicken.

"Great time. How are you guys?"

"Good, my husband is getting drunk off eggnog," she pointed out, and Shea laughed, holding up his cup to cheers with Karson.

Doing so, Karson laughed as Shea drained his cup.

"I'm living it up. We said bye to the kids, and after this, we are heading to the hotel for crazy monkey sex before leaving in the morning for Fiji," Shea said with an unstoppable grin.

His captain was good and toasty drunk.

"What he means to say is we will have sloppy sex, and then he'll oversleep and bitch the whole way to Fiji. I am so excited I can't stand it," she corrected and Karson laughed.

His boss might be a tad bit drunk too, but he wasn't going to point that out.

"You guys are a riot," he declared, and they both beamed at him.

"Where's that wife of yours?" Shea asked.

"She's getting food…oh, here she is," he said when Lacey showed up beside him with no food. "Where's the food?"

"I didn't want anything."

"Where's my turkey leg?"

She shook her head. "No, it was gross."

Karson glared as Shea said, "No, man, go get one. I've eaten like three of them."

Lacey laughed as she pointed to him and asked Elli, "Is he drunk?"

Elli nodded. "Damn eggnog gets him every time."

They all laughed and talked for a little longer before Karson found himself on the dance floor with his sexy wife. She had natural rhythm, and he loved moving against her as the lights glittered above them. Holding her close, he kissed her jaw as the music changed to a soft love song. Looking deep into Lacey's eyes, he felt nothing but undying love for her. Things had been nuts with her family but they'd overcome it. He had his claws in her, and she wasn't going anywhere without him. He loved her so much, and the thought of not having her honestly murdered him. She was his everything.

His forever.

When his phone started to vibrate in his pocket, he pulled it out to see it was Kacey.

"It's Kacey."

"Eek! Answer it!" she said before dragging him off the dance floor and to a quiet area of the party.

Putting his phone on speaker, he said, "So?"

Kacey laughed. "So you are speaking to the newest member of the US women's hockey team!"

"WHOOOOO!" Karson yelled out as Lacey cheered loudly. Everyone turned to look at him and he hollered, "My sister made the US women's team!"

Everyone cheered and Kacey giggled. "Oh my God, way to make a girl feel special!"

"You are! I can't wait to watch you kick ass. We'll come up, right, babe?" he asked as the adrenaline coursed through his body. His sister was going to play in the Olympics!

"Of course. Oh my goodness! We are so proud of you, Kacey!"

"Thanks, guys. I love you, but let me let you go. I've got things to tend to."

"Damn jerk, I'm trying to congratulate you!"

"Oh, shut up. I've got billions of people to call. You were first!"

Lacey smacked him and shook her head before saying, "Okay, congrats!"

"Love you, Kacey, really proud of you," he said, and he was surprised by the tears that were itching his eyes. He was on the ultimate high.

"Love you, Karson, and you too, Lacey. Thank you! I'll call you guys later."

Karson was grinning ear to ear as he hung up and looked down at his beautiful wife.

"Man, that made my night," he said, bringing Lacey in close. "I'm so proud of her."

"I am too."

Kissing her jaw, he closed his eyes and couldn't believe it. He was beyond blessed. Not only was his family doing well, but he was completely and utterly in love with the most gorgeous woman ever. Yeah, it took nine years to get everything he wanted, but now that he had it, he was never letting go.

"I think I have something that is going to make it ten times better though," she said, looking up at him, her eyes sparkling with tears.

His brow came up. "I mean, if you are talking about that ass and me getting it in the bathroom, then yeah, I think you do have something that can make it ten times better."

She laughed. "No, dork. Something else."

He looked at her questioningly. "I don't need anything else. Just looking at you makes my night."

She smiled, kissing his jaw before taking his head in her hands and putting her lips right by his ear. "I love you."

"I love you more," he answered, wrapping his arms tightly around her waist.

She kissed the spot below his ear and then said, "I'm pregnant, Karson."

Everything stopped as he just stood there. Pulling back, he looked down to see that tears were rolling down her cheeks, and the biggest, most gorgeous grin was on her beautiful face.

"Pregnant?"

She nodded. "You've been trying harder than I think you've realized."

He laughed as his heart exploded in his chest. "We are going to be parents."

Her lip quivered as the tears rushed down her cheeks. "We are. I just found out this morning, and Karson, I am so happy. Scared out of my mind, but I know you'll be there. You'll coach me through this scary thing, and together, we will be the best parents any child ever had."

"Damn fucking right, come here, baby," he said, pressing his lips to hers in a frenzy. Moving his lips with hers, tears stung his eyes as his heart went insane in his chest. He had waited for this moment his whole life. He'd wanted to have children with Lacey since he met her, and now they were doing it. They were going to be parents. The best damn parents in the world. He would get to watch her grow their child; he would love her and make sure that she knew she was gorgeous all the damn time. Shit, how did he get so damn lucky?

Pulling away, he kissed her lips again before saying, "It's me, you, and now our baby nugget."

She laughed as she nodded. "Forever."

"Forever," he agreed.

And forever never looked as good as it did in that moment, and he really wasn't sure how any holiday was ever going to live up to his first with Lacey.

But he was excited to try.

"Thanks, guys. I love you, but let me let you go. I've got things to tend to. Oh, shut up. I've got billions of people to call. You were first! Love you, Karson, and you too, Lacey. Thank you! I'll call you guys later."

Hanging the phone up, Kacey let out a breath and smiled. She was an Olympian. She was going to fight for the gold for her country, and she couldn't fathom how this had happened. Yeah, she worked hard and she wanted it, but wow, she was going to do it.

When she felt lips along her spine, she looked back at her lover and smiled.

"You do have things to tend to," Jordie said roughly against her back.

She knew it was a bad idea to come to see him, but she needed him. She was nervous about the phone call and wanted to lose herself while she waited. Jordie Thomas was the best distraction for that. His body was a wonderland of hard muscle and sex. He could have her flat on her back in seconds with only a smile. She loved him.

Which was very stupid.

"Mmm, what do I have to tend to?"

"Me," he said, laying her back and slowly getting on top of her. He was slow because of his leg, but when he got in her, slow was good. He was big. Very big and it hurt, but it was a good hurt, one she craved. "I want you, my sexy little Olympian."

She smiled widely before his mouth covered hers, his hand coming behind her knee to open her up to him. Pulling away from her mouth, he kissed her jaw, nibbling at her neck before trailing kisses down her stomach. She wasn't sure how this happened. At first it was to get back at Karson for calling her gay, but then when she was in bed with Jordie, being fucked to the point of no return, she liked it. A lot. And continued to come back for him. She knew it was stupid, but Jordie Thomas made love like a god.

Her body quivered in anticipation as he kissed her flat belly and her mound before opening her up and feasting on her. Running his tongue along her lips, he took his time, almost as if he was worshipping her pussy, driving her completely mad. When the tip of his tongue slowly traced around her clit, she almost came off the bed, crying out his name. Relentlessly, Jordie devoured her pussy, making her cry out things she never had before. He had that power. He brought out the animal inside her.

And when she came, she didn't just orgasm. She flew. Rocketed through space as she came. Her whole body seized and she found herself unable to breathe as he kissed her pussy, her thighs, and whispered such wonderful things.

"You are so beautiful, so damn beautiful. I could stay between these thighs for days."

As he kissed up her body, his beard tickled her chest before his mouth met hers in a fevered kiss. "I can't get enough of the taste of you," he whispered against her lips as he slowly moved inside of her, filling her completely. "The feel of you...you drive me crazy, Kacey."

Closing her eyes, she moaned out his name as he pushed inside her, taking her breath, her existence, her everything.

"So fucking beautiful," he grunted as he thrust in and out of her, his body heavy on hers. They had been doing this for a month, and in that month, she had fallen completely in love with him. He was funny and sweet but also an asshole, challenging her. She loved messing with him and then getting punished later. He was amazing, but he was clear that they were just fucking. She couldn't help but think maybe that was changing though. Especially with the way he looked at her. Like she was important and special.

Hating how much she cared, that she had fallen, she pushed into his chest, and he went onto his back like she wanted. Going on top of him, she directed his large cock inside of her, and as every inch of him disappeared, she closed her eyes, loving the feel of him completely inside of her. Taking ahold of her hips, he moved her roughly up and down him, her ass smacking against his thighs as she rode him into oblivion. When she came, she squeezed him so hard, he couldn't breathe as he came, his fingers bruising her hips.

Gasping for breath, she looked up at the ceiling and knew this had to stop. Every second she stayed with him, she fell harder, and that couldn't happen anymore. It wasn't fair to her or him. He would feel bad because he did care for her, but he would never love her. He couldn't. He wasn't made to do that; he didn't have the chemical makeup to trust anyone, and she understood that. Accepted it, and she had to get away because she wouldn't even be able to be his friend.

Looking down at him, she smiled as he moved his thumb along her nipple, the other hand holding her tightly.

"You're gorgeous, Kacey King."

"You aren't too bad yourself," she answered back, leaning down to press her lips to his. Bracing her hands at the sides of his head, she looked deep into his brown eyes and decided she was really going to miss him. "This is the last time, Jordie."

His brow came up. "No, I plan on making you come at least three more times tonight."

She scoffed. "You wish. You don't make me come; I choose to."

He laughed. "Baby, don't test me. I'll throw you up on my face and have you coming in seconds."

Her body was engulfed in flames at the thought, but she reined it back in. That wouldn't happen. She'd never leave if it did. "Maybe."

Jordie chuckled. "Are you challenging me?"

"No, shit. Shut up," she said, setting him with a look before kissing him deeply. When she got off him, that was it. They were over. Never again would she find herself in Jordie Thomas's bed. Pulling away, she gazed at him as he looked up at her, confused.

"What is it, Kacey?"

"This is it. This is goodbye. We can be friends because I do enjoy picking at you, but we can't sleep together anymore."

His eyes held hers as he asked, "Can I ask why? I like what we do."

"Oh, I do too, but I've caught feelings."

His eyes went wide but he recovered quickly, looking up at the ceiling, his thumb stopping at her nipple. "Caught feelings, huh?"

"Yeah, I love you, and while I know that horrifies you," she said since she could see it all over his face, "I know the score. I know this was supposed to be just fucking, but somewhere in there, I fell for you. So, yeah. I gotta stop this before it gets so bad that I can't walk away."

Glancing away, he moved his hand down his face. "I wish you wouldn't have done that. I like this. A lot. You. I like you, but I can't love you."

"I know," she said with a nod and slowly got off him, patting his chest. "And I'm not mad. Hurt, yeah, because I could see us having a good life together, but it's not you."

She got up, but he took her hand, stopping her. She met his gaze and pushed back her tears as his eyes searched hers. She expected him to tease her, to lighten the mood, but instead, he said, "I wish I could."

"Me too," she whispered before swallowing past the lump in her throat. She got dressed in silence as he watched. It took everything not to cry, but she wouldn't. She couldn't. She wouldn't show weakness. As she went for the door, he took her hand, and she was surprised that he had gotten out of bed. His leg was still pretty messed up and it was hard for him to walk, but soon he had his arms around her, his lips at her neck as he hugged her tightly. Kissing her jaw, he then took her lips with his, kissing her long and hard, curling her toes in her boots.

Pulling back, he looked deep in her eyes. "Karson isn't gonna come after me for hurting you, right?"

She shook her head quickly. "No, I promise. I knew the score. This is my fault."

"I was just joking. I owned up to being with you."

"Oh, okay."

Lifting her chin with his finger, he looked deep into her eyes and whispered, "I'm gonna realize one day that I shouldn't have let you go, and I'm pretty sure I'm gonna regret it. By then though, you'll find some schmuck who will love you the way you deserve, and you'll be happy. That's what I want."

Her lip quivered as she looked down at his bare chest, the scars of his past screaming at her. He'd had it so hard growing up; the scars weren't just internal, they were even visible. She got it. She got him; she just wished it would end differently.

"But if, for some reason, you haven't found him, you better believe you will be mine, Kacey King. There won't be any stopping that."

Smiling, she looked up at him and said, "That might be the only time I'll let you win."

His grin was infectious as he nodded. "I always win."

Kissing his jaw, she had to get away before she lost it. He kissed her once more, and then against her lips, he whispered, "Know that you're the only girl who has left a mark."

She nodded. "I wish that mark was enough."

"Me too," he admitted, but she knew it wasn't. He wouldn't trust someone enough to love them. He couldn't. Kissing him once more, she opened the door and shut it before walking away as fast as she could to make sure he didn't come after her. She didn't want him to see her cry. She wanted him to think they ended things and her heart was intact, but that wasn't the case. As she rushed to the car, she didn't cry because they were over, she cried because it happened and she knew she'd never be the same.

Looking at the clock, she saw that it read midnight, which meant the new year was here. She had heard from Lacey that the person you are with on New Year's is the one you'll be with for the next year. Well, she was alone, crying in her damn car.

Wonderful.

"Happy fucking new year to me."

Happy Holidays!

My amazing readers,

Thank you for reading this novella and I hope it brought some holiday cheer into your heart. I know that Kacey's story didn't end very merrily, but that just gives a chance for her story to continue. Look forward to **Overtime,** *coming spring 2015, to see if Kacey gets her Happily Ever After.*

I love y'all so much and I couldn't do this without you.

Thank you & Happy Holidays!

Love,
Toni.

Upcoming from Toni Aleo!

Becoming the Whiskey Princess (Taking Risk Novel 2) January 2015
Clipped by Love (Bellevue 2) February 2015
Overtime (Assassins 7) April 2015

And a brand new series is coming in Summer 2015 from Toni Aleo
The Spring Grove Novels
Bring on the cowboys!

Make sure to check out these titles and more on Toni's website:
www.tonialeo.com

Or connect with Toni on
Facebook: www.facebook.com/tonialeo
Twitter: twitter.com/toniloveswebere6
Goodreads: www.goodreads.com/author/show/5255580.Toni_Aleo
Instagram and more!

Also make sure to join the mailing list for up to date news from the desk of Toni Aleo:
http://tonialeo.us6.list-manage.com/

Made in United States
Troutdale, OR
11/18/2024